NEXT STOP: SPANISH

Keith Massey

Lingua Sacra Publishing

Next Stop: Spanish
Copyright © 2009 by Keith Massey

Published in the United States by Lingua Sacra
Publishing.
www.linguasacrapublishing.com
ISBN 978-0-9843432-1-8

Dedication

To my wife.

Acknowledgements

With thanks to Sean Sullivan for his helpful comments on the project.

About the Author

Keith Massey, Ph.D., is the author of *Intermediate Arabic for Dummies*. He is a former linguist with the National Security Agency and is currently a language instructor.

Legal Disclaimer

The views and opinions expressed in this work are the author's and not that of The National Security Agency or the U.S. Government.

INTRODUCTION TO NEXT STOP: SPANISH

Now, the story I'm about to tell you will include an unexpected adventure that, in many ways, changed my life. But it is also the story of how I started learning Spanish. My uncle, whom you'll meet soon, taught me some Spanish using a method he himself designed. It gives one a basic speaking ability by focusing on the most essential words and phrases you need. But it still requires a bit of work on the part of the learner.

If you want to join me fully on this adventure, you should try to learn along with me. As a part of this story, I'll be describing times when I needed to study the next installments of words my uncle gave me. My uncle's advice to me was to write out the English and Spanish in my own handwriting and then read the lists out loud to practice the words. There will also be times when you encounter Spanish in this book without understanding it completely. Join the club. But my uncle told me over and over again to just try and understand what you can. If you even just write out the lists of words once and try to follow this story, you'll be starting down the path of learning Spanish. And as I tell the story, I will be using more and more Spanish within it, as we both learn and become more comfortable with the language.

A few comments on how to pronounce Spanish. First of all, you can listen to all the words and phrases you will learn in this book on the author's website. But here's a rough idea of how to pronounce Spanish. Most vowels and consonants are pronounced the same as English. Here are the ones that are different:

A is pronounced like the O in *on*.

C is a hard K (as in <u>c</u>ard) before A, O, and U, but an S sound before E and I.

E is like the AY in *bay*.

G is a hard G (as in <u>g</u>ame) before A, O, and U, but a rough H before E and I.

H is silent.

I is like the EE in *feel*.

J is a rough H.

LL is pronounced like Y.

Ñ is pronounced like the NY in *ca<u>ny</u>on*.

QU is pronounced as K.

R is trilled.

RR is a long trill.

Z is pronounced like S.

Buena suerte, dear reader. That's Spanish for "Good luck!"

CHAPTER ONE

A jet roared overhead as the main terminal appeared around a curve. As I looked up, I saw wisps of white cloud beyond the plane in a brilliant blue sky.

"You have your passport, right?" my dad asked.

"You saw me put in my bag," I answered, laughing.

"He's just nervous since you've never left the country," my mom said, running her hand through the hair on the back of my dad's head. His premature gray seemed especially white against the deep black of his cassock. As an Orthodox priest, he wouldn't absolutely have to wear the formal garb at all times. But that's my dad's way.

"Do you guys even know where Uncle Andrew is taking me?"

"Somewhere Spanish speaking, I assume," he said.

"I just thought since you and he talk on the phone at least once a day he might have let it slip."

"He wants it all to be a surprise for you," my mom said, turning around with a huge smile. "He's kept it a surprise even from his twin."

"And he knows how to keep a secret," my dad said.

We all laughed in the knowledge of my uncle's particular background. As a former linguist with the National Security Agency, he was once in on lots of highly classified material that he can't divulge even now.

My dad pulled up in front of a set of large glass doors. A sign overhead was marked with the name of my airline. We all piled out to head for the trunk.

"Here you go, John," he said, putting the strap of my single carry-on over my shoulder. It was my only luggage, since I like to travel light. My father kissed me on each cheek, in the tradition of his Romanian heritage. "Call us as soon as you land in Washington."

"I will."

My mom hugged me and then kissed my forehead. "You're going to have a great time. I know this is all about studying, but don't forget to have some fun, okay?"

"Yes, mom. And you two enjoy the cruise!"

She smiled. "I'm a little nervous about getting seasick, but we'll have fun. You get going now."

"Alright. Call us later," my dad repeated, stepping back toward the driver's door of the car.

"Okay. Bye." Turning toward the terminal building, I saw the automatic doors open to my approach. Once inside, I spotted a mercifully short line for check-in. Just a few minutes later, I was approaching the desk.

"Hi there," I said, putting my driver's license and the sheets I printed from the internet on the counter.

"Good afternoon," responded a blue-uniformed woman with a nod. She took my materials and began furiously typing at her keyboard. "It's just you travelling today, Mr. Valquist?"

"Yes," I replied. "Could I have an aisle seat if one's available?" Reading her badge, I spotted that her last name was Villalobos. Even though she spoke with no hint of an accent, I realized then that she did have vaguely Hispanic features.

"One passenger flying to Reagan International?" she confirmed, setting my identification and other sheets back in front of me.

"Yes," I said, chickening out on a momentary impulse to respond in what little Spanish I already knew.

She handed me a paper envelope containing my boarding pass. "I've got you confirmed and ticketed, aisle seat as requested."

I remembered that my uncle had asked me to promise that I would use Spanish as much as possible on this trip. "*Gracias*," I said.

She lit up with a huge smile. "*¿Habla español?*"

"Well, that's about as much as I know right now," I said. "But I'm going to Washington to study it with my uncle."

"*Buena suerte*," she said, nodding. "Good luck."

"*Gracias*."

"*De nada*."

An escalator brought me toward the security checkpoint. Walking slowly toward the growing line of passengers, I put my wallet, keys, and phone in a side pocket of my bag. Even thought I had never flown internationally, I had gotten plenty of experience in it during flights to visit colleges during the past several months.

Once beyond the metal detector and x-ray machine, I settled into a seat by my gate. I extracted a manila folder from my bag and began looking at two pages of Spanish language materials that had come as an attachment in an email from my uncle. I leaned back in my chair and took a deep breath, releasing it in a sigh louder than I intended. I hate studying. So why was I spending the final week before I started college subjecting myself to a Spanish language boot camp? Sitting there looking at those pages, I needed to remind myself why I agreed to do this.

I have never been any good at languages. Two years of French early in high school had left me with little more to show than "*bonjour.*" My dad had tried off and on to teach me Romanian, which gave me little more than "*bună ziua.*" What I was very good at, however, was baseball. I was ranked as the top pitcher in Ohio my senior year and received a full scholarship to the University of Virginia. Unfortunately, I would still need to take two years of a language for my degree. I couldn't bear to think of going back and starting over in French. So Spanish seemed the most logical choice, and I was already registered to take Spanish 101 in the fall semester. When my uncle found out about all of this, he and my dad crafted this plan for me to jump start some Spanish abilities before school started. It all seemed like a fine idea a few months back. But now here I was, sitting in an airport looking at my first homework assignment since graduation two months earlier.

I reread the letter Uncle Andrew sent me.

"This is 'Phase One' of your Spanish studies. Try to know what's on these pages well before your arrival. And be able to tell me the Spanish for 'I need help' when you see me."

A clock on the wall told me that I still had an hour before boarding. It was just enough time to make at least a dent in this work. Despite the initial shock of seeing how much I was supposed to study, I was relieved to notice that I already knew many of these words and phrases:

Greetings and Phrases

Hello
Hola

See you later
Hasta luego

Goodbye
Adiós

I took a deep breath and continued studying:

Good morning
Buenos días

Good night
Buenas noches

Good afternoon
Buenas tardes

Please
Por favor

Thank you	no / not
Gracias	*no*
You're welcome	maybe
De nada	*quizás*
Excuse me	and
Perdóneme	*y*
yes	or
sí	*o*

Following my uncle's advice, I took out a notebook and began the task of merely copying the list of greetings out, in both English and Spanish. I did notice that even concentrating momentarily on them went a long way towards teaching me the few items I was not familiar with, like *perdóneme* and *quizás*.

My uncle had also told me that I was supposed to read all of this out loud after writing it down. Just to make sure that I was pronouncing everything correctly, I listened on my MP3 player to a file my uncle sent in which he read the whole list out loud. As I started, I read it first in a very hushed voice. I guess I was nervous that the other people would think I was crazy to be talking to myself. But I relaxed a bit about it and raised my volume when I saw that no one around me seemed to be bothered.

I had just finished a second read-through of this section when the attendant at my gate came onto the loud speaker.

"Boarding all rows for flight 407 with direct service to Washington."

Packing up my things, I proceeded down the gangway and settled into my seat on what turned out to be a sparsely occupied flight. I had the aisle seat and no one had the window. Once airborne, I set out all my materials in the seat next to me and headed into the rest of the words and phrases I was supposed to study before arrival:

Do you speak English?
  ¿Habla inglés?

I don't speak Spanish very well.
  Yo no hablo español muy bien.

"*¿Habla inglés?*" I said, repeating the phrase. "*Yo no hablo español muy bien.*"

"That's okay," a woman's voice said, pushing a beverage cart up the aisle from behind. "I speak English."

I turned a bit startled and saw a flight attendant smiling broadly. Her deep brown and curly hair and the name Maria on her name badge explained her response.

"I'm going to Washington to study Spanish with my uncle," I said.

"That's nice," she said. "*Buena suerte.*" Maria continued pushing the cart up the aisle and began dispensing drinks. Judging from the number of rows, I decided I had just enough time to at least begin working through the rest of the phrases:

Please speak more slowly.
  Por favor, hable más despacio.

Please repeat that.
  Por favor, repita eso.

I'm sorry, but I don't understand.
  Lo siento, pero yo no lo entiendo.

How do you say that in Spanish?
  ¿Cómo se dice eso en español?

What does that word mean?
  ¿ Qué quiere decir esa palabra?

It seemed that my uncle was giving me precisely those statements I would need if I began bravely using my Spanish as he suggested. I wrote them all out and gave the sentences a listen before starting to read them out loud to myself. Next came some basic verbs:

Basic Verbs

I am
  Yo soy / Yo estoy

I go / I will
  Yo voy

I have
  Yo tengo

I know
  Yo sé

I like
  Me gusta / Me gustan

I think that
  Yo creo que

I need
  Yo necesito

Could you ... ?
  ¿Podría Usted ... ?

I want
  Yo quiero

I'd like ...
  Me gustaría ...

I can
  Yo puedo

I had just finished writing out this batch of words when Maria returned.

"What would you like to drink?" she asked.

I realized I knew enough to attempt the exchange in Spanish. "*¿Como se dice* 'Water with ice' *en español*?"

"*Agua con hielo,*" she said.

I repeated her words carefully and softly. Looking at my list, I added what she told me to one of the sentences there. "*Me gustaría agua con hielo.*" I smiled with excitement at having created an entire sentence. "Oh, *por favor*," I added.

"*Claro*," she said, giggling and preparing the beverage. "*Aquí la tiene*," she said, handing me a plastic glass and a napkin. She set a bag of pretzels on my tray and continued on her duties.

Energized by the exchange, I pressed forward in my studies. All that was left of "Phase One" was a list of the pronouns and some basic numbers:

Pronouns

I *Yo*	we *nosotros*
you (sing. informal) *tú*	you (pl. informal) *vosotros*
you (sing. formal) *Usted*	you (pl. formal) *Ustedes*
he *él*	they *ellos*
she *ella*	

Numbers

number *número*	five *cinco*
zero *cero*	six *seis*
one *uno*	seven *siete*
two *dos*	eight *ocho*
three *tres*	nine *nueve*
four *cuatro*	ten *diez*

It relieved me to be done with the first installment of my studies, but then I remembered my uncle's assignment. I was supposed to say "I need help" in Spanish when I saw him. I had learned that *yo necesito* means "I need," but several scans through Phase One did not give me the final piece of the puzzle. I was momentarily worried I would not be able to complete the task when I remembered that Maria would certainly know the word.

A few minutes later she was returning to the front of the plane.

"*Perdóneme*," I said upon her approach.

"*Sí?*"

"*¿Cómo se dice* 'help' *en español?*"

"*Ayuda*," she replied.

I quickly wrote it on my sheet. "*Gracias*," I said grinning.

"*De nada.*" She continued toward the front of the plane.

I pushed the button on my armrest and reclined my seat. Closing my eyes, all I saw were Spanish phrases in my own handwriting scrolling through my mind. A few minutes later, I slipped into a restless nap.

A nudge on my arm suddenly pulled me into a groggy consciousness.

"We're getting ready to land," Maria whispered. "Please put your chair back in the upright position."

"*Sí*," I said, still disoriented.

"*Bueno*," she said with a smile. "You're starting to think in Spanish."

I nodded and complied with her request. Looking out the window, I saw we were already quite close to landing. Maria had apparently let me sleep until the absolute last second she could. A moment after seeing fields and trees, we were descending upon nothing but city. In the distance, a flash of white caught my eye. I focused on the source and spotted the unmistakable spire of the Washington Monument. A flutter of wonder and pride surged in my heart. Even though I had been to Washington on a number of occasions to visit my uncle, the national monuments have never failed to move me. A few minutes later and we were on the ground.

From within the crowd of bustling passengers, I flung my bag over my shoulder and filed past the pilot and Maria standing at the door.

"*Gracias*," I said. "Your *Ayuda ... me gusta*," I added, knowing that I had not produced anything close to a correct Spanish utterance.

"*De nada*," she responded, unfazed.

I was beaming as I walked through the doors and off the airplane. Even though I knew so little at that point, it felt good to use Spanish to connect with people. The feeling made me want to know even more.

On previous trips to visit my uncle, I had gotten used to taking the metro which runs straight from the airport to a stop not far from his house. As I walked down the terminal in the direction of that train station, I opened my cell phone to inform him of my safe arrival.

"*Yo soy* ... um ... here," I said, hearing him pick up.

"*Muy bien*," he answered. "I'll be waiting for you at the stop."

"That's Huntington Station, right?"

"*Sí*," he said. "*Hasta luego. Adiós.*"

I heard a click and stuffed the phone in my shirt pocket. Following the signs toward the metro stop, I continued through several series of halls, their floors gleaming with a fresh polish. Several minutes later, I stepped into the broad space of the station itself. A wind was swirling through the area as I saw my subway roar along the tracks and slow to a stop. I stepped onto the brightly lit train. Since I knew I had only four stops, I decided to stay standing and just held onto one of the chrome bars. As we travelled, I called and talked to my mom and dad to let them know I had arrived safely. I knew that since they would be going on their cruise the following day, I wouldn't talk to them again now for a week.

After ten minutes, I emerged at Huntington Station in Alexandria, Virginia. As soon as the escalator had brought me to ground level, I spotted my uncle. Before me stood a mirror image of my father — the same medium height, late thirties, and prematurely gray hair — but in a tan tweed jacket instead of a black cassock.

"So good to see you, John," he said, kissing me on both cheeks in the Romanian style.

"*Yo necesito ayuda*," I said, in fulfillment of his request.

"*Fantástico*," he replied. "Did you look up the missing word on the internet?"

"I got it from one of the flight attendants."

"Even better. *Vámonos*. Let's get going," he said, stepping toward the curb.

I turned and saw what I recognized as his compact black car parked directly in front of us. I opened the passenger side door and got in.

"Are you hungry?" he asked, getting behind the wheel and pulling the door shut.

"*Sí*," I said. "But anything you want is fine by me."

He looked over his shoulder and pulled us into traffic. "Then you're okay with ordering in some pizza?"

"*Bueno*," I replied.

We drove quickly into an area that was quiet and thick with trees. As we drove in darkness through ever more narrow streets, I saw the orange glow of muted lights in the houses on each side of us. The size and apparent value of the homes gradually grew as we made what I remembered as the turn onto my uncle's street. With a sharp turn on the wheel, my uncle pulled the car into his driveway.

In the light of a half moon, I saw his large and vine covered brick house. "I still don't understand how you afford a place like this on the salary of a Latin teacher," I said.

"They pay me more than I deserve," he replied.

We quickly unloaded from the car. I followed my uncle through the front door of his house and immediately smelled a burning fireplace.

"Let's get you settled in your bedroom," he said. "Then you can get washed up and relax a bit."

I continued after him as he proceeded through the unlit foyer. The bare hardwood floors creaked in whispers as we turned to the right and ascended a winding staircase onto the second floor of the palatial estate.

"You're here on the first left," he said, opening the door and switching on a light.

I saw swirls of purple paisley patterned wallpaper. The king sized bed in the center of the room matched the color scheme.

"I've redecorated this room since you were here last," he said.

"It's nice," I replied, realizing why my mother is in charge of furnishing back home.

"Listen, you get settled in and cleaned up. Your bathroom is the room straight across the hall. You've got towels and everything else you need in there. I'll call for our dinner so it will be here in about an hour."

"Sounds good, Uncle Andrew."

He smiled and left the room.

I took a quick shower and changed into a t-shirt and sweatpants. Collapsing on the bed, I closed my eyes for a few minutes. I still could only see waves of words pouring across my mind's eye. Since I knew he had only given me Phase One of probably several more, I felt a momentary shudder of depression that my time with my uncle would be dominated by this project. I like my uncle and I enjoy spending time with him, but I was facing the prospect of a week-long mental fatigue in his presence.

I sat up and took a deep breath. The recollection of why we had come up with this plan returned. I needed to come away from this trip more relaxed about the semester of Spanish that I would be taking. My training depended on me taking as many stresses as possible off my mind. And so, I turned and put my feet on the floor, a bit recharged for the journey ahead.

As I circled down the stairs to the first floor, I heard the doorbell ring. My uncle arrived at the foyer just before me.

"This is the pizza I ordered for us," he said, taking out his wallet. He opened the door to reveal a man standing with a large box. "*Buenas tardes, Jorge,*" my uncle said, apparently already on a first name basis with the delivery man. "*Aquí tiene veinte dólares y el resto es para Usted.*"

I understood the word *dólares* to mean "dollars" and assumed *resto* meant "rest." Given what usually happens in a pizza delivery, I deduced that my uncle had given him an amount of money and told him to keep the change. But I was very impressed at how nice of an accent my uncle spoke in.

"*Muchísimas gracias, Señor Valquist,*" the man said with a gentle smile. "*Adiós.*"

We went into the kitchen. I saw plates already arrayed on the table.

As I pulled out a chair and sat down, I saw several beverage options arranged before me. My uncle poured himself a glass of red wine and sat down.

"I suppose you're wondering about our itinerary," he said.

"It's crossed my mind," I chuckled. "Acapulco? Cancún?"

"Madrid."

"Wow," I said. "I've never been to Europe."

He looked at the glass of wine he had poured for himself. "Now, John, since you're eighteen, you could choose to drink wine when we're over there. But you'll understand that I can't let you have any here tonight."

I laughed. "That's quite fine, uncle. It doesn't fit into my training regimen." I poured myself a glass of sparkling water and dragged a large piece of pizza onto my plate.

"Our flight leaves tomorrow mid-afternoon," he said, taking a piece himself. "So tomorrow morning, we'll have you start work on Phase Two."

"And you really believe just one week will help me pass Spanish?"

He nodded. "You'll see, John. I've crafted my program over several years to provide the learner with exactly the words you need to be comfortably proficient. Before we come home from Spain you'll tell me that you feel good about that class."

"Sounds great." I took a few bites off my pizza and set it down. "What else are we going to see besides Madrid?"

"Well," he started. "There's plenty to do in Madrid itself. But we're also going to get out for a few excursions. You'll even meet a former colleague of mine who will also be in Spain."

Now my Uncle Andrew had never talked much about his time with the NSA. I always wanted to hear some of his war stories.

"So this is a friend from your former spy days?" I asked, hoping to get privileged information.

He looked at me over his glass as he took a sip. "The gentleman you'll meet is currently an agent with MI-5. How and where I made his acquaintance is top secret."

"MI-5?" I asked excitedly. "That's Bond's agency, right?"

"Oh, I assure you that the life of an intelligence officer is ordinarily not that exciting."

"But you did have some adventures, right?" I asked.

He smiled and sighed. "It was something very exciting to have done," he said. "And yes, I did things and went places I never in my life could have imagined. But now I'm happy to just be a mild mannered Latin teacher."

"That is unless this Latin teacher job is just an elaborate cover for something else."

He raised an eyebrow. "And just what can you imagine an NSA agent would be doing undercover at a private academy specializing in Latin?"

"It's a strange world out there," I said.

We both laughed.

After the pizza, we sat in the living room and relaxed. My uncle turned on a Spanish language channel on the TV and let it play softly in the background while we chatted. All along I was also wanting to see the scores of several baseball games I knew were happening that day, but I stayed with him.

At ten o'clock my uncle got up. "It's time for bed," he said. "I'll be waking you up very early."

"How early are we talking here?"

"Try four."

"Ouch. Is there a reason?"

"By my experience, we'll get over jetlag in Spain easier if we start moving our body clocks in the direction of Europe even tonight."

"Will there be coffee?" I asked seriously.

"Of course. And right after coffee and breakfast ... "

"*Yo sé*," I said. "Phase Two."

"*Sí*," he said.

I got up myself. "Then, *buenas noches*, uncle."

"*Buenas noches, Juan.*"

CHAPTER TWO

I did not sleep well that night and had been awake for maybe half an hour when the sound of my uncle's alarm clock blared distantly through the walls. I heard him moving around the house for a few minutes before he came to wake me up. He gently tapped at my door.

"John?"

"I'm awake," I said, struggling to sit up. "I'll be down in a minute."

I put back on the clothes I was wearing the previous evening and carefully stepped down the staircase, hoping coffee was waiting for me. The smell of a freshly brewed batch greeted me. I felt a little better already.

"Here you are," Uncle Andrew said, setting a cup in front of me. "Anything in it?"

"Just a little milk," I said.

"*Un café con un poquito de leche*," he said. He poured it in so the fluid came directly to the brim. I leaned over and sipped enough to make it stable.

"I'm betting you didn't sleep too well last night," my uncle said.

"How did you know?" I asked.

"The first night doing some significant language work will usually clutter your brain enough to rob you of good rest. Don't worry, though. It'll pass soon."

"That's good to know." I took another deep sip off my coffee.

"And then tomorrow you'll have sleep disruption all over again from the jetlag."

"Excellent."

"What would you like for breakfast?" he asked. "I've got various cereals or I can make us some eggs."

"Eggs would be great," I said. "I need to eat a lot of protein because of my workout level."

"While I get that ready for us, you should start reading into Phase Two."

I nodded. "As long as there's refills on coffee."

He chuckled. "*Por supuesto.*"

Uncle Andrew began going back and forth between the refrigerator and the stove in preparation for the meal. I saw several sheets of paper sitting on the table in front of me.

"Phase Two, I presume?"

"*Sí.*"

"A few questions," I started.

"*Sí?*"

"*¿Cómo se dice* 'uncle' *en español?*"

"*Tío,*" he said, cracking eggs and pouring them into a bowl.

"*Tío, como se dice* 'coffee' *en español?*"

"*El café,*" he answered.

"*Me gusta el café,*" I said, smiling and holding up my cup.

He stopped work for a moment and turned toward me. "Why have you told me that you don't have any linguistic ability? Getting new words so you can use them is exactly what one has to do in order to succeed. You've been selling yourself short."

I sipped my coffee. "My dad couldn't teach me Romanian. And I did terrible at French."

"Romanian is an extremely difficult language. Your dad and I grew up speaking it every day."

"Why did my grandma make you two learn Romanian? You were born here in the United States."

My uncle laughed. "What has your father told you about her?"

"Only that she defected back in Communist times."

"She had the dream of going back to Romania some day. And she wanted us to know Romanian in case that ever happened."

"That was before the accident."

"Right," he said.

I noticed that tears had formed in my uncle's eyes. "I wish I could have met her," I said.

"Your dad and I were your age when our parents were killed. And Communism ended just one month later."

"She'd be very proud of what her sons became," I said.

"She certainly would," he returned. "Anyway, as for your French, your poor teacher was likely saddled with a daily mountain of administrative duties and the challenge of teaching to a room of kids who don't want to learn. It wasn't your or your teacher's fault that you didn't take to French."

"I suppose."

"Alright, I have to get to work on breakfast. Study!" He turned back to the counter and started whipping the eggs.

I looked at the next installment of sentences:

Phrases

What is your name?
  ¿Cómo se llama Usted?

My name is ...
  Me llamo ...

"*¿Cómo se llama Usted?*" my uncle asked, knowing the first phrases I was looking at.

"*Me llamo John,*" I replied. "*¿Y cómo se llama Usted?*"

"*Me llamo Andrew.*"

I continued into the phrases. Remember that if you write these out yourself, you can learn words and phrases of even long lists like this one:

Nice to meet you.
  Mucho gusto.

How are you?
  ¿Cómo está Usted?

I'm fine
  Estoy bien

So-so
  así-así

Where are you from?
  ¿De dónde es Usted?

I'm from ...
  Yo soy de ...

Where is the ...
  ¿Dónde está ... ?

What time is it?
  ¿Qué hora es?

How much does that cost?
  ¿Cuánto cuesta eso?

Where do you live?
  ¿Dónde vive Usted?

I live in the United States.
  Yo vivo en los Estados Unidos.

I'm an American.
  Yo soy americano.

I read the phrases several times and proceeded into the nouns:

Nouns

the man	the woman
el hombre	*la mujer*

Since my uncle was just then putting sausage links in a heated frying pan, I knew we had a few minutes until breakfast was ready. "*Tío*, can you explain the different forms of the word 'the' that I'm seeing here?"

He turned and nodded. "The word for 'the' in Spanish is just a little more complicated than in English. Every noun is either masculine or feminine. Feminine singular words use *la* for 'the'. To make plural in Spanish, you add '*s*', just like in English. If a word ends in a consonant, add '*es*'. Make sure you add the '*s*' or '*es*' to both the noun and the word for 'the'. So how would you say 'the women'?"

I looked at the item on the list. *Mujer* ends in a consonant, so I needed to add '*es*'. "*Las mujeres*?"

"Right."

"How do I know if a noun is feminine?" I asked.

"For now, if it describes a female or ends in an '*a*', it's feminine. You'll learn more word endings that are always feminine in coming days."

I nodded. "And the masculine?"

"Masculine nouns have '*el*' for 'the' in the singular and '*los*' in the plural. And you'll add an '*s*' to the noun when you use '*los*'. So tell me, how would you say 'the men'?"

I applied what he told me. "*Los hombres?*"

"*Sí.*"

"And words are masculine if they describe a male," I said. "Any other rules?"

"Words that end in '*o*' will almost always be masculine. But there are words that don't end in '*o*' that are masculine too. Don't worry about details this early in your studies. What I've just described is enough to start playing with adding the word 'the' to things. Let's do a little more practice on this. The way you say house in Spanish is *casa*. Add the word 'the'."

I thought through the rules he had told me. It ended in '*a*' and so it was feminine. "*La casa.*"

"Good. Now make it plural. The houses."

"Just add '*s*' to the article and the word itself. *Las casas.*"

"Excellent. *Libro* means book."

"Ends in '*o*', so it's masculine," I said. "*El libro*. Plural would be *los libros*."

"Nicely done, John. One more easy lesson. The masculine word for 'a' or 'an' is *un* and the feminine version is *una*. Tell me how to say 'a book'."

"*Un libro.*"

"*Bueno*," he said. "A house?"

"*Una casa.*"

"*Excelente, Juan.* Breakfast will be ready in about ten minutes."

"I'll study until then."

I continued into the nouns:

the person	the table
la persona	*la mesa*
the thing	the house
la cosa	*la casa*
the place	the bathroom
el lugar	*el cuarto de baño*
the chair	the name
la silla	*el nombre*

Food and Drink

the food	the water
la comida	*el agua*
the drink	the bread
la bebida	*el pan*

I saw that my uncle was almost done with our breakfast. "*Y me gustaría la comida,*" I said, putting together some of the things I had learned.

"*Yo también*," he said, starting to scoop scrambled eggs onto the plates. He added a few sausage links to each and we headed into our breakfast. While we ate, I continued studying more of the words:

Adjectives

good
  bueno

bad
  malo

nice
  simpático

pretty
  bonita

handsome
  guapo

sick
  enfermo

tired
  cansado

happy
  contento

sad
  triste

right
  derecha

left
  izquierda

this
  esto

that
  eso

big
  grande

small
  pequeño

"So most adjectives are masculine?" I asked. "I mean, they end in '*o*'."

"I give you the masculine form in the lists, but if they end in '*o*', you change it to an '*a*' when it describes something feminine. So a sick man is *un hombre enfermo*, but a sick woman is *una mujer enferma*."

"What about the ones that don't end in '*o*', like *triste*?"

"Those don't change. Quiz time. The small house."

"*La casa pequeña.*"

"The big thing."

"*La cosa grande.*"

"You got it."

As I looked at the words and the ones still to come, I began to worry about how I would remember so much new information. "Any advice on how to learn all these words?" I asked.

"Just keep doing what I recommended. Write everything out in your own hand."

"Why exactly?"

"For some reason, the human brain absorbs information more efficiently when it's in your own handwriting. It's something about how the brain stores it. This method has been known and written about for two thousand years."

"If it works so well, shouldn't I use it for all my courses?" I asked.

"Absolutely," he said. "That's why your teachers have you take notes. But with language it's particularly important."

We finished eating and my uncle set me up at a desk upstairs, so I could continue to work on Phase Two.

"Stop when you get to the verbs," he said. "I want to explain some things before you study them."

"Excellent," I said. "I better get started.

I could hear him cleaning up the kitchen and then packing. I wrote out everything I had looked at that morning into my notebook and then continued to the new words:

Time

the time
  el tiempo

the hour
  la hora

the day
  el día

the night
  la noche

the morning
  la mañana

the afternoon
  la tarde

the evening
  la tarde

yesterday
  ayer

today	now
hoy	*ahora*

tomorrow	then
mañana	*entonces*

I quizzed myself on the addition of the word "the" using what I guessed were a feminine and a masculine noun. *Hora*, "hour," produced *la hora*, "the hour" and *las horas*, "the hours." *Nombre*, "name" gave me *el nombre*, "the name" and *los nombres*, "the names." I smiled in pride at my new found ability.

I read on:

Interrogatives

who	why
quién	*por qué*

what	how
qué	*cómo*

where	how much
dónde	*cuánto*

when	how many
cuándo	*cuántos*

My uncle must have known that I was getting toward the end of Phase Two.

"Remember to save the verbs until we get to the airport," I heard him call upstairs.

"*Sí, tío!*" I called back. I continued into some prepositions:

Prepositions

in	of
en	*de*
with	from
con	*desde*
to	for
a	*para / por*

I studied a miscellaneous collection of basic words and some more numbers:

Miscellaneous

here	really
aquí	*de veras*
there	very
allí	*muy*

also
  también

well
  bien

but
  pero

again
  otra vez

together
  juntos

of course
  por supuesto

Numbers

eleven
  once

seventeen
  diecisiete

twelve
  doce

eighteen
  dieciocho

thirteen
  trece

nineteen
  diecinueve

fourteen
  catorce

twenty
  veinte

fifteen
  quince

twenty-one
  veintiuno

sixteen
  dieciséis

As I wrote out these words, I realized that I could now make sense of what my Uncle Andrew had said to the pizza delivery man the previous night. "*Aquí tiene veinte dólares y el resto es para Usted.*" I had learned in just Phases One and Two most of the sentence. *Aquí* means "here." *Veinte* is "twenty." *Y* means "and." *El resto* is a masculine noun. The plural would be *los restos. Para* means "for" and *Usted* is the formal way to say "you."

Since my brain needed a rest, I was happy that my uncle had told me to wait on the verbs. I left the study and found him in his room putting things in a suitcase.

"*¿Qué hora es?*" I asked from my phrase list.

"*Son las diez y media,*" he said.

I searched the word list in my brain. *Diez* means "ten" and *media* reminded me of the word "middle," so I assumed it was 10:30. "When do we need to leave here?"

"*A las once,*" he said. "You've done everything but the verbs?"

"*Sí, tío.*"

"Then go take a break and make sure your luggage is all ready. Double-check that you have your passport."

"You're just like my dad!" I laughed and left the room.

I set my luggage by the door and collapsed in a large leather armchair in the living room. My brain was swirling with words. I began to feel the fatigue of my bad night. Just as I closed my eyes to see if I could catch a bit of a nap, I heard the doorbell ring.

"Get that, would you?" my uncle called from upstairs. "That's our ride to the metro station."

"Sure," I said, struggling out of the chair. I opened the door with no expectations about what I might see there. You'd think that would mean I couldn't be surprised. What I could not have anticipated was seeing a man who looked like he could beat up the Incredible Hulk. In front of me was a six and half by four foot wide block of muscle.

"Hi," the man said. "I'm Nick, the gym teacher at your uncle's school. You must be John."

I stepped back to let him in the door, which I was almost surprised he got through without needing to turn sideways. "You're the gym teacher?" I asked. "What did you do before that? Green Beret or something?"

"Navy Seal," he said seriously.

I shook my head. This school of my uncle's was certainly an enigma.

"Hey, Andy, you ready?" the man shouted.

My uncle came down the stairs with a single carry-on.

"Is that all you're packing?" Nick asked.

"Why bring a set of clothes for every day when there will be a sink to wash them in?" He smiled. "Let's go, gentlemen."

We got in Nick's Hummer and a few minutes later we were back where my uncle had picked me up the previous evening.

"Thanks, Nick," my uncle said. "I'll give you a call when we get in next Sunday."

"Sounds good," he said. "*Buena suerte*, John."

"Does everyone in the world speak Spanish except me?" I asked with a laugh.

We retraced my trip on the subway and arrived back at the airport. As we got up to the check-in counter, I cringed to see a line of several dozen people waiting to be processed for our plane.

"I guess we should have gotten here a little earlier," I said.

"Come with me," he said.

I followed him to the First Class counter, where he presented our passports.

"Are you serious?" I asked. "We're on First Class?"

"Well, I can't go back to Business Class, John. So here we are."

"Let me get this straight. You're the Headmaster at a Latin school where the gym teacher is a former Navy Seal and you fly First Class everywhere you go."

"Your point?" he asked.

I shook my head. "Oh, nothing."

The attendant handed us our boarding passes and we were on our way. Shortly after clearing security, my uncle turned toward a set of large glass doors.

"Where are you going?" I asked.

He smiled. "To the First Class lounge!"

We passed through the doors and my uncle showed our tickets to a woman at a large marble desk. She stamped them and smiled.

"Leave your bags with us, gentlemen. Enjoy your stay. We'll call you when your plane is boarding."

I shook my head in disbelief at the level of service. "I didn't even know this place existed."

We entered the lounge itself and I saw a full bar and several rows of buffet with every imaginable type of food.

"I'm a bit hungry," I said. "Is this free for us in here?"

"Oh, we paid for it," my uncle said.

"Well, someone paid for it," I countered. "I still suspect that it's the taxpayers."

"Get something to eat and then let's finish off the verbs before we take off."

I gathered a selection of foods, everything from egg rolls to sliced prime rib. When I came to where my uncle was sitting he was sipping a glass of red wine.

I sat down on the couch beside him. "I'm bracing myself for this," I said. "Verbs must be really hard."

He laughed. "Thank God you're not learning Latin. Spanish is easy in comparison."

"My dad told me that your students actually learn to speak Latin. Is that true?"

He nodded. "Yes, as well as Spanish, French, Italian, and a smattering of Greek."

"Why are they actually learning to speak Latin?" I asked. "No one does that today."

"It's an excellent foundation for learning other languages."

"Or this is still all part of the elaborate cover story."

He smiled. "All you need to remember is that the ending of the verb changes depending on who is doing the action. And so, *tengo* means 'I have'. You can add the pronoun you learned in Phase One if you want and say *yo tengo*. But *tengo* all on its own will mean the same thing."

"I can accept that."

"*Tiene* means 'he or she has'. So add the pronoun and say 'he has'."

I recalled my pronouns from Phase One. "*El tiene.*"

"She has."

"*Ella tiene.*"

"*Muy bien,*" he said. "Now write out and try your best to learn the four basic verbs for Phase Two. I give you all the forms along with their pronouns. The first form you see — the one that always end in 'r' — is called the infinitive. It means "to do something." In other words, *tener* means 'to have' and *querer* means 'to want'."

I took a deep breath and released it. "Alright, here I go."

Scanning the forms he supplied, I began my verb study. First came the full lists of four important verbs:

Basic Verbs

ser, to be

I am
yo soy

we are
nosotros somos

you (sing. informal) are
tú eres

you (pl. formal) are
Ustedes son

you (sing. formal) are
Usted es

they are
ellos son

he/she is
él/ella es

estar, to be

I am
yo estoy

we are
nosotros estamos

you (sing. informal) are
tú estás

you (pl. formal) are
Ustedes están

you (sing. formal) are
Usted está

they are
ellos están

he/she is
él/ella está

querer, to want

I want
  yo quiero

you (sing. informal)
want
  tú quieres

you (sing. formal) want
  Usted quiere

he/she wants
  él/ella quiere

we want
  nosotros queremos

you (pl. formal) want
  Ustedes quieren

they want
  ellos quieren

tener, to have

I have
  yo tengo

you (sing. informal)
have
  tú tienes

you (sing. formal) have
  Usted tiene

he/she has
  él/ella tiene

we have
  nosotros tenemos

you (pl. formal) have
  Ustedes tienen

they have
  ellos tienen

After I wrote them, I read them out loud several times. I turned to my uncle. "Quiz me on these," I said.

"Alright. What do you put on a verb when the action is done by 'you' informal singular?"

"An 's'. But what are the formal and informal ways of saying 'you'?"

"You use *tú* forms only with family, close friends, and children. Use *Usted* forms with people you don't actually know."

"Alright."

"What is the ending for verbs done by 'we'?"

"*Mos.*"

"They?"

"An *n.*"

"But you notice that sometimes there's an extra *y* after the *o*."

I nodded. "Like *estoy* and *soy*. How do I learn all this?"

"Don't worry about why there are these little irregularities right now. That's the difference between learning the language and learning about the language. Even back in Phase One you learned a few verbs as vocabulary items only. It's enough for now to know that 'I can' is *yo puedo* and the way you say 'I know' is *yo sé*. You don't need to know why they don't have the same ending."

"But this is exactly the kind of thing I can remember being quizzed on in French," I said.

"I'm sure," he said. "Your poor teacher had to have something to use as the basis for giving grades. But that doesn't mean it's the best way to learn a language."

I chuckled. "I get your point. What's the story with two verbs that mean the same thing? *Ser* and *Estar*? They both mean 'to be'. Help me."

"You'll study this in more depth when you take your class. But I can summarize it for you like this. You will use the verb *estar* when you describe how something feels or where it is."

"Okay, so I say *estoy aquí* - I'm here - not *soy aquí*."

"You use *ser* to describe what something is."

"*Soy un hombre.*"

"Quiz time. I'm sick."

I thought for a moment. That's a feeling. "*Yo estoy enfermo.*"

"I'm in the house," he said.

Where I am. I need to use *estar*. "*Yo estoy en la casa.*"

"I'm a student."

What something is. "*Yo soy* ... um ... *¿cómo se dice* 'student' *en español*?"

"*Estudiante.*"

"*Yo soy estudiante.*"

"You rule."

"Can I take a break now?"

"You're so close to being done, John. Just finish the infinitives and then take a break."

I began my study of these things he was calling infinitives:

Verb Infinitives

to be
  ser, estar

to say
  decir

to do/make
  hacer

to think
  pensar

to go
  ir

to know
  saber, conocer

to be able
  poder

to want
  querer

to eat
  comer

to need
  necesitar

to drink
  beber, tomar

to have
  tener

to speak
  hablar

to like
  gustar

"What's the difference between *saber* and *conocer*?" I asked. "They both mean 'to know'."

"*Conocer* is to know or to be familiar with people or places. *Saber* is for everything else, facts, information, skills, etc."

"Gotcha. When do I actually use infinitives?"

"They complete the action for verbs like *querer* and *poder*. You learned the *yo* forms of those verbs back in Phase One. 'I want to eat' is *yo quiero comer*. 'I can speak' is *yo puedo hablar*."

"Make me do one."

"I want to go to the house," he said.

I thought of what I needed to say. "*Yo quiero ir a la casa.*"

"I can think."

"*Yo puedo pensar.*"

"Well done, John. You can use *voy*, which means 'I go' to create the future tense with an infinitive."

"I remember that in Phase One *voy* meant 'I go' and 'I will'."

"The only difference is that you add the preposition *a* before the infinitive. So 'I will have' is *yo voy a tener*. 'I will say' is *yo voy a decir. Y ahora dígame cómo se dice en español* 'I will speak'."

"*Yo voy a hablar*," I answered.

"Nice. 'I will go'"

"*Yo voy a ir.*"

"Excellent, John."

After I was done writing out all these forms into my notebook, I sat back. "Now can I take a break?"

"I insist on it," he said. "We're going to be getting on that plane soon and I want you to relax, watch movies — flirt with flight attendants if you want. But don't study formally until about an hour before we land. Then, just read through all that you've done."

"That's a deal," I said. "When you say 'formally', do you mean I should study informally?"

"The reason we're flying on a Spanish airline is to ensure that our flight attendants speak Spanish. Just have some fun and see what you might be able to accomplish if you're sitting in absolute luxury with nothing to lose."

I smiled. "We'll see what kind of trouble I can get myself in."

A gentle intercom called us by name and informed us that First Class boarding of our flight would be beginning soon.

"*¿Vamos a España?*" my uncle asked.

"*Sí.*"

As we entered the First Class cabin, I was shocked to see just six seating stations spaced widely through that section of the plane. One passenger had already turned his chair into a half-bed and was relaxing with a glass of champagne.

"What would you like to drink?" a tall and slender woman dressed in a scarlet dress suit asked me in excellent and only slightly accented English.

"*Me gustaría ...* " I was embarrassed to realize that I knew how to say 'I would like' but I didn't know how to say the thing I wanted. "*Perdóneme*," I said, glancing at her name badge — another Maria. "*¿Cómo se dice en español* 'Cola'?"

She giggled. "*la palabra es* 'Cola'."

"It's the same thing," I said.

"*Sí.*"

"*Me gustaría Cola, por favor, Maria.*"

"*En seguida, señor.*"

My uncle had heard the exchange and not intervened. "Nice job of working your Spanish. I forgot to tell you that in the event you don't know a word, just go ahead and say the English. And sometimes it'll be the same anyway."

"So I've learned."

She returned with my drink and set it on a wide table between our seating stations.

"*¿Y para Usted, señor, qué le gustaría?*" she said to my uncle, apparently picking up the vibe that he spoke Spanish.

"*Me gustaría un vaso de vino tinto seco, Cabernet, si tiene.*"

"*En seguida, señor.*"

"*En seguida* means something like 'Coming right up'?" I asked.

"*Exactamente.*"

"That's how you say 'exactly'?"

"*Sí.* Here's a little bonus lesson for you. You can turn a large number of English adverbs into Spanish just by changing the 'ly' into *'mente'*. "

"Give me an example," I said.

"If the adjective ends in an '*o*', change the ending to '*a*' and then add '*mente*'. If it ends in anything else, just add '*mente*'. Got it?"

"*Sí.*"

"The word for 'frequent' in Spanish is *frecuente*. How do you say 'frequently'?"

Doesn't end in '*o*'. Just add '*mente*'. "Frecuentemente."

"The Spanish word *rápido* means 'fast' or 'quick'. How do you say 'quickly'?"

Change the '*o*' to '*a*' and then add '*mente*'. "*Rápidamente*?"

"Good. 'Possible' is *posible*."

"*Posiblemente*?" I said.

"You've got it, John. You're getting good at all this."

"Well, to be honest it's because I have an excellent teacher."

"*Gracias, Juan.*"

"*De nada.*"

"One more thing," I said. "How come there are two words that mean 'for'? I just heard *para Usted* and *por favor*. What's the difference between *para* and *por*?"

My uncle nodded. "I'm sorry I forgot to discuss it. It's not really something you can put into a single sentence explanation. At this stage just don't worry about it."

"I'm going to trust you, but when I'm taking my class you can give me a detailed lesson, right?"

"It's a deal."

Our plane took off just a little late. I strained to pull even a word or two out of the Spanish version of the in-flight announcements but certainly didn't understand it. My uncle informed me that competent second language speakers of English can't usually follow English language news either; it's just too fast. This encouraged me.

A half an hour into our flight, Maria delivered menus for us to choose our dinner orders. In First Class, you get a choice of entrees. This also gave me the chance to practice my Spanish a bit more.

"What would you like, sir?" she asked.

"*Voy a España*, ah, to practice *español. ¿Podría Usted hablar español* with me?"

"*Sí. Qué quiere, señor?*"

"*Me gustaría ...*" I read off the menu. "*El pollo y papas fritas.*"

"*Y para beber?*"

I had just learned that *beber* means 'to drink'.

"*Un vaso de Cola, por favor.*"

"*En seguida, señor.*"

"*Gracias ... para ... estar ... bonita.*"

She blushed and turned to her duties.

My uncle cleared his throat. "Um, right above *'bonita'* in your list is the word you were trying to remember."

"Oh right," I said. "I wanted *simpático* — I mean the feminine form *simpática*. But instead I said ... "

"Thanks for being beautiful."

I was mortified. "What do I do here? Should I apologize?"

He laughed. "Let me take care of it."

Maria returned delivering drinks to the passengers in the cabin.

"*Perdóneme, señorita. Mi sobrino está aprendiendo español y no tuvo la intención de usar la palabra 'bonita'. Quiso decir 'simpática'.*"

"*Oh, entiendo, señor. No es un problema.*"

"*Pero, en hecho, señorita, ambas palabras son verdaderas para Usted.*"

She smiled and purred as she retreated to the galley.

"Wow," I said. "I didn't follow hardly any of that apart from the fact that you were totally coming on to her."

"All this too can be yours, John. Just keep studying."

After dinner, I starting watching a movie on my personal TV screen, but fell asleep in the middle of it. I woke up just once as Maria was spreading a blanket over me.

"*Gracias*," I whispered half-asleep. "*Usted es muy simpática.*"

CHAPTER THREE

I don't know how long I slept on that flight. My uncle said it was only about two hours, but it felt like much longer. And I awoke feeling so mentally charged that I did something I could not have imagined just two hours earlier.

"Where's Phase Three?" I asked my uncle, rubbing my eyes.

He put down the in-flight magazine which somehow had his interest. "I thought we decided that you would wait until tomorrow morning after getting to Madrid?"

"The more I learn the more I want to know. I want to be able to relate to people even better."

"Ah ha!" my uncle exclaimed. "You've just found the ultimate secret to learning a language."

"And what's that?"

"Motivation. People who learn a language because they want to interact with others have far and away the best long term outcome in their studies."

"Alright then," I said, sitting up. I pressed the button which began converting the bed into a chair. "I want to get started."

Uncle Andrew extracted another several sheets of paper from his briefcase and handed them to me.

"As always, I'm here for questions."

"*Gracias.*" I looked at another collection of phrases:

Phrases

My father is a nice man.
  Mi padre es un hombre simpático.

This man is tall.
  Este hombre es alto.

It was fun to try and guess just from the phrases
what the main grammatical lesson of each phase would
be. It seemed that adjectives and how to use them
could be a working title here. I continued in the
phrases:

My car is bigger than yours.
  Mi auto es más grande que el tuyo.

I have no idea.
  No tengo ninguna idea.

Are all your friends here?
  ¿Están todos sus amigos aquí?

I learned many things from him.
  Yo aprendí muchas cosas de él.

That woman is beautiful.
  Esa mujer es bonita.

I saw my friend's new house yesterday.
Yo vi la casa nueva de mi amigo ayer.

Tell me something new.
Dígame algo nuevo.

I think that this shirt is better than that one.
Pienso que esta camisa es mejor que ésa.

I'm hungry.
Tengo hambre.

I'm thirsty.
Tengo sed.

As I wrote out the phrases, I was noticing that the adjective was sometimes following the noun it described and other times coming before. I assumed that there was a rule my uncle could explain to me. I came up with my own working theory that adjectives follow the noun with the exception of the words like "this," "that," "all," and "many."

"*Mi tío*," I said, looking over at him, "I was hoping you could clarify where to put adjectives like *esta*."

He took a sip from a glass of wine and nodded. "Basically, put adjectives after the noun with just a few exceptions."

"Like *mucho*, *esto*, and *todo*."

"*Exactamente*."

"I rule."

"Now, I notice that verbs like *aprendí* and *vi* have different endings than the ones you taught me yesterday. Is that because they're past tense?"

"*Sí*," my uncle replied. "But you're only learning the past tense within phrases for now."

"When will I learn the past tense formally?"

"Sometime later in your first semester."

"But isn't it important to be able to talk in the past?"

He got up from his chair and stretched. "It is. And you'll be learning some important past tense verbs within some phrases. That's better than learning the past tense as a theory and then trying to generate past tense verbs."

"This sure is a different way to learn than anyone else uses," I said.

He smiled. "Your fortune for having an uncle who was trained to be a spy."

I laughed and turned back to the word lists. I saw a continued cascade of important and basic nouns:

Nouns

the people
la gente

the girl
la niña

the boy
el niño

the husband
el marido

the wife	the brother
la esposa	*el hermano*
the father	the sister
el padre	*la hermana*
the mother	the friend
la madre	*el amigo*
the son	the family
el hijo	*la familia*
the daughter	
la hija	

I processed these words into my notebook and suddenly felt my strength to continue fading quickly. It felt, in fact, as though anything more I tried to do would not be accomplishing anything. My uncle must have seen my fatigue.

"You know, there's a reason I call them 'Phases' and not 'Days'. Why don't you leave the rest of Phase Three for tomorrow morning? Your brain can't properly acquire language unless you are well rested. Keep that in mind for next year in college too."

"Good idea," I said, putting the materials away. "*Y ahora yo quiero* to watch a movie."

As I rewatched the film I had fallen asleep during, they brought back up the lights and we were served breakfast. It's a strange feeling how an international flight compacts an entire day into a seven hour block of time. Feeling a little charged by coffee and an exquisite omelet, I decided to head back into my studies:

Food and Drink

the coffee
  el café

the beer
  la cerveza

the tea
  el té

the wine
  el vino

the milk
  la leche

I was happy to see here words that I had already learned, like *el café*, and other words that would not be too difficult to learn, like *el té*. I even remembered that my uncle had used the word *la leche* when he put milk in my coffee the previous day. This all encouraged me, because I realized that long lists of new words didn't need to scare me since they would probably contain things I had already learned.

I explored some more adjectives:

Adjectives

my
mi

our
nuestro

your
tu

their
su

his
su

her
su

much/many
mucho/muchos

few
pocos

all
todo

none
ninguno

new
nuevo

young
joven

old (people and things)
viejo

more
más

less
menos

better
mejor

worse
peor

"Tell me something, *mi tío*," I started.

"*Bueno. ¿Qué quieres?*"

"All these words seem so obviously important, like you can't really say you know the language until you learn them."

"That's true."

"How many words does one have to know before you can say you actually speak a language?"

He put his magazine down and looked up in thought. "It's more a philosophical question than a linguistic one. I would argue that if you know so much as one word, you are a quantum leap ahead of someone who knows nothing."

"But that's not the same as knowing the language. I want to be fluent in this language. How long will that take?"

"Americans tend to fail in learning languages because they have an unrealistic view of fluency. Europeans learn just enough of ten languages to get by and consider that *knowing a language.*"

"How will I know when I actually *know* it?"

He nodded. "That will be for you to decide."

I chuckled. "That has kind of a Zen quality to it. I like it."

We were told to put our seats in their upright position and to prepare for landing. As we lowered our altitude, I saw an arid and mountainous region with scattered collections of houses in the valleys.

"Are we going to visit this area?" I asked. "It looks awesome down there."

My uncle craned his neck to look out the window. "I wasn't planning on us coming out here. Apart from Madrid I saw us going to a beach on the Mediterranean."

I smiled. "You're right, the mountains can wait for another trip."

A few minutes later, the wheels of our plane bumped to a landing at the Madrid International Airport. We gathered our bags and lined up to exit the plane. Maria was standing at the door to see passengers off.

"*Gracias por todo,*" I said.

"*De nada,*" she replied. "*Tenga un buen viaje a España.*"

I smiled and nodded even though I had only caught the words *buen* and *España*.

"*Si está Usted libre esta noche para la cena, llámeme más tarde,*" my uncle said, handing Maria a slip of paper.

She took it hesitantly and put it in her pocket.

As we walked up the gangway, I turned to my uncle.

"Did you really just give that woman your phone number?"

"Wouldn't it be nice if Maria could join us for dinner tonight?"

"Especially because I'd excuse myself early to go study."

"Ah, so you know the code?"

"Fluently."

As we emerged into the terminal itself, I saw an explosion of Spanish words everywhere. I don't know why I had not expected this.

"You've now officially started the immersion part of your language learning experience. Even if you don't use Spanish for everything you say, you're going to be hearing hours and hours of Spanish for the next week."

"How could I get this experience if we weren't travelling to Spain? I mean, how can I recapture this later in the semester?"

"Do what I did last night and just turn on some Spanish channel and listen to it."

"But I couldn't follow any of that. It's just too fast."

"It doesn't matter. Listening to language even when you're picking out stray words is still valuable. That's how you'll spend the rest of this week here."

"Alright, Sensei."

As we approached the passport control, I stopped my uncle. "Hey, how come words like 'passport' don't appear in one of the earlier Phases? Don't I need it for travel purposes?"

He laughed. "This is another reason why Americans don't learn languages. Half the books and programs out there teach you unnecessary words connected to travel encounters like customs and shopping when these are precisely the places where you can count on someone knowing English."

"*Pero, ¿cómo se dice* 'passport' *en español?*"

"*Pasaporte.*"

"Yeah, not necessary for my lists."

We continued through the passport control. As we entered the main reception lobby, I immediately saw a man in a suit holding a placard reading "Valquist."

"That's me," my uncle said.

"Nice to meet you, sir," the man said, shaking his hand. "This is John? Nice you to meet you." He extended his hand and we shook.

The man took our bags and headed toward the exit doors.

"Is this a friend of yours?" I asked.

"It's a driver from a car service I use here."

"How come we have the luxury of a car service here and we took the metro to the airport in Washington?"

My uncle smiled. "I like to pamper myself when abroad."

I shook my head. "There's a lot I don't understand."

For a half an hour we cruised back and forth between large multilane streets and unbelievably small back streets and arrived in front of what might have been a house, were it not for the canopy over the front door advertising it as a hotel.

Our driver jumped out and got our bags from the trunk and set them on the sidewalk in front of the hotel.

"Thank you," my uncle said. "We'll see you again on Sunday morning."

"Yes, sir," he said, getting back in the car and pulling away quickly.

"Don't we pay him?" I asked.

"Already taken care of."

We entered the hotel lobby and saw a tall white marble counter.

"*Buenos días*," an elderly gentleman said. "*En qué puedo ayudarles*?"

"I heard *ayuda*," I said. "How can I help you?"

"*Exactamente*," my uncle said. "And you learned *puedo* already in Phase One. Notice how you're able to understand normal exchanges after just a few days of study?"

"It's awesome."

My uncle stepped to the counter and set a sheet of paper in front of the man. "*Tengo una reservación para dos personas por seis días*."

"Reservation is *reservación*?" I asked.

"*Sí*. We'll talk about that a bit later."

The man quickly handed us a set of electronic keys.

"*Están Ustedes en doscientos y uno. El ascensor está a la derecha, allá*." He pointed down a hallway.

"*Gracias*," I said.

We walked down the hall and found the elevator on the right. On the second floor, we found our room, number 201. I swiped the key and entered first. There I saw a large living area with a full kitchen and separate bedrooms coming off the main space.

"Are you kidding me?" I asked. "What's this place costing?"

"*Yo no sé exactamente*," he said, setting his bags down on the floor. "Before I forget, I want to talk about *reservación*."

"Right."

"Virtually every word in English that ends with 'tion' or 'sion' exists in Spanish with the ending '*ción*' or '*sión*'. In English we pronounce both endings 'shun' and in Spanish both are pronounced like 'see-on'. And you always throw the accent on the final syllable."

"Give me another example."

"There are hundreds. English 'nation' is *nación* in Spanish. 'Demonstration' is *demonstración*. So tell me how to say 'indication' in Spanish."

I thought through the transformation. "*Indicación*."

"Tension."

"*Tensión*. And that one would even be spelled the same."

"Option."

"*Opción*."

"In other words, John, you already have a vocabulary in the hundreds for Spanish, as long as you practice converting the English you know into Spanish words that are almost identical."

"One more," I said anxiously.

"A long one. 'Fortification'."

"*Fortificación*."

"And they almost always exist."

"But not always?"

"Over ninety percent will be there when you create them."

"I like those odds. Are there other word types that work like this?"

"Plenty," he said. "But let this one sink in today. Ask me tomorrow and I'll walk you through a few more."

"You also used both *para* and *por* in that sentence downstairs. Any explanation for why the difference?"

My uncle chuckled. "You can't stand not knowing how things work. *Tengo una reservación para dos personas por seis días*. It's *para* because it's for our benefit — *para dos personas*. But it's *por* with frequency or time, so 'for six days' — *por seis días*."

"I still don't think I would know which one to choose on the spot."

"That will come in time."

I nodded and sat down on a couch beside a fireplace. "What's on our agenda for today?"

He opened the minibar and took out a bottle of mineral water. "*Ahora son las diez. Tienes hambre*?"

"*No.*"

"Then I propose you finish up Phase Three and then we'll get a nice lunch somewhere."

"Agreed."

I took out the sheet and continued my work. More important words were added to my inventory:

Time

the second	never
el segundo	*nunca*
the minute	sometimes
el minuto	*a veces*
the week	often
la semana	*a menudo*
the month	once
el mes	*una vez*
the year	twice
el año	*dos veces*
always	soon
siempre	*pronto*

I studied a miscellaneous section of important words:

Miscellaneous

because	much
porque	*mucho*

a little 　*un poco*	already 　*ya*
enough 　*bastante*	nothing 　*nada*
only 　*solamente*	something 　*algo*

I got the full present tense for some of the infinitives I had learned the previous day:

Basic Verbs

saber, to know

I know 　*yo sé*	we know 　*nosotros sabemos*
you (sing. informal) know 　*tú sabes*	you (pl. formal) know 　*Ustedes saben*
you (sing. formal) know 　*Usted sabe*	they know 　*ellos saben*
he/she knows 　*él/ella sabe*	

poder, can, to be able

I can
yo puedo

we can
nosotros podemos

you (sing. informal) can
tú puedes

you (pl. formal) can
Ustedes pueden

you (sing. formal) can
Usted puede

they can
ellos pueden

he/she can
él/ella puede

necesitar, to need

I need
yo necesito

we need
nosotros necesitamos

you (sing. informal) need
tú necesitas

you (pl. formal) need
Ustedes necesitan

you (sing. formal) need
Usted necesita

they need
ellos necesitan

he/she needs
él/ella necesita

gustar, to like

I like
me gusta/gustan

we like
nos gusta/gustan

you (sing. informal) like
te gusta/gustan

you (pl. formal) like
les gusta/gustan

you (sing. formal) like
le gusta/gustan

they like
les gusta/gustan

he/she likes
le gusta/gustan

I turned to my uncle. "*Gustar* isn't like the other verbs at all. What's the story with it?"

"Technically *gustar* means 'to please', and the object of the verb is the one pleased by something. So the way you say 'I like the food' in Spanish is to say, literally, 'the food pleases me', *me gusta la comida.*"

"And 'you like the water' would be *te gusta el agua*?"

"Right. If the thing you like is plural, you use the *gustan* form, since the think you like is actually the subject of the verb. So how would you say 'we like the books'?"

I found the forms in my mind. "*Nos gustan los libros.*"

"You got it. You have just the infinitives left?"

"Yes, and I'll be ready to eat after that."

I turned back to the sheets and learned a few more verb infinitives:

Verb Infinitives

to ask	to hear
preguntar	*escuchar*
to answer	to understand
responder, contestar	*entender*
to tell	to take
decir	*tomar*
to give	to use
dar	*usar*
to come	to leave
venir	*salir*
to see	
ver	

I wrote all of these words out fully into my notebook. I read through the whole of Phrase Three twice and then went back and read through all of Phases One and Two. I'd advise you to go back regularly and review everything you've learned so far also. Eventually, you'll see like I did that the earlier material becomes second nature by the repetition.

I put my materials away and sat back on the couch. "*Tengo hambre ahora, mi tío.*"

"*Yo también,*" he said. "*¿Qué quieres comer?*"

"*Estamos en España, mi tío. Necesitamos comer comida española!*"

"*Bien,*" he said. "Now, just to warn you, Spanish food is not Mexican food like you might know from the States."

"You'll recommend something nice, I'm sure."

"*Vámonos, Juan.* No more formal studying until tomorrow morning. Even if you beg me for Phase Four, I'm not giving it to you."

"It won't happen."

We got back on the elevator and left the hotel. My uncle turned to the left and seemed to know where he was going, so I didn't even ask what was in store for lunch.

"I notice that your cell phone hasn't rung yet," I said. "Do you suppose Maria was weirded out by your offer?"

"*¿Quién sabe?*" he asked. "It's early yet."

We arrived at a sidewalk café with tables arranged along the red brick wall of the building. The sky was free of clouds but the sun did not seem overbearingly bright.

"Is this it?" I asked.

"*Sí.*"

A waiter arrived and handed us two menus. "*Siéntense, por favor,*" he said. "*Vuelvo inmediatamente.*"

"*Gracias,*" I said, taking the seat facing out toward the sidewalk.

"Your dad always let me take the 'guy's seat' since he's already married."

"Well you've got competition now, *mi tío.*"

"*¿Cómo se dice* 'competition' *en español,*" he said.

"*Competición,*" I replied.

"*Bueno.* What are you in the mood for?"

"*Comida. Mucha comida.*"

The waiter returned. "*¿Podría traerles una bebida primero?*"

I understood *bebida* and *podría* and was able to guess at the purpose of the question. "*Sí, quiero beber un* ... (I didn't know the word for "lemonade," so I guessed) *lemonado.*"

"*Una limonada,*" the waiter said, understanding me and saying what would have been correct. "*Con hielo?*"

Now I was clueless. "*Mi tío, que quiere decir hielo?*"

"Ice."

"Oh snap!" I said. "I learned that word just two days ago. *No, señor, gracias. No hielo.*"

"*Bien. Y para Usted?*"

"*Para mí, una limonada con mucho hielo,*" my uncle said.

"*Y han decidido para la comida?*"

"*Todavía no,*" my uncle said.

"*Regreso inmediadamente con las bebidas*," the waiter said and returned inside.

"I can't wait for the day when I follow everything that just happened there," I said.

"Don't focus on what you don't know," he said. "You've been studying Spanish for three days and the most important thing anyway is to be brave and creative with what you do know."

"I know," I said. "So what are you getting us for lunch?"

"*Te gusta* fish?"

"Honestly, not much."

"The Spanish word for 'honest' is *honesto*," he said, looking over the menu. "How would you say 'honestly' in Spanish?"

As I thought through the conversion, I noticed a woman in a dark blue dress suit across the street look away suddenly and press her ear, as if listening to an earpiece.

"Um, *honestamente*," I said slowly. "Is there any chance you and I could be under surveillance?"

"The woman across the street?" my uncle asked, not looking up from his menu.

"You noticed her too? Alright, well, now she's coming this way."

"Just be natural."

The woman crossed the street and approached our table. She produced a wallet from her suit jacket and flipped it open to reveal some type of badge.

"Excuse me, Dr. Valquist," she started. "I'm with CNI. Could I speak with you for a moment?"

"*¿Qué es* 'CNI', *tío*?" I asked.

"It's the Spanish equivalent of the CIA or NSA."

"I would like to speak with you away from here," she continued. "I'd like you to come with me to our headquarters immediately. I believe you may be in some imminent danger."

The sudden sound of tires squealed from down the street.

"Get on the ground!" my uncle shouted, knocking me off my chair and piling over me beside the table.

Gunshots rang out from a car that raced by. I heard ricocheting bullets hit the restaurant wall above where we had been sitting. The woman dove to the sidewalk and rolled toward the street. She pulled a pistol from her jacket and fired at the car as it now raced away.

"*Codo rojo! Codo rojo!*" the woman shouted. In a second, two more suited men had appeared from the nearby crowd and were aiming pistols around the perimeter.

"Are you okay?" my uncle asked insistently.

"I'm fine."

"Listen," my uncle said. "We're leaving with these people. Get ready to follow me."

"Who shot at us?"

"*Yo no sé*," he said.

A van braked to a halt on the street in front of us.

"Dr. Valquist, move out!" the woman shouted.

He got up and took my hand, pulling me to my feet. I followed him as he ran toward the back of the vehicle. The woman took up a position next to the door and continued sweeping her pistol across the scene. As my uncle pushed me into the back of the van, I saw two soldiers inside, wearing camouflage and holding black rifles.

"Sit down," my uncle said, climbing into the van himself. "And hang on!"

As the woman jumped in, the doors were slammed shut from outside. The next instant, I was knocked off my seat by the rapid acceleration. I struggled back to a seated position as I felt the vehicle taking sharp turns.

Just that moment, my uncle's cell phone rang. He looked at the agent, who gave him a nod. He pushed the button and put the device to his ear.

"*Sí?*" he said, looking at me, listening and forming a smile. "*Lo siento mucho, Maria, pero desafortunadamente no estoy disponible hoy.*"

Despite still being gripped with panic from what had just happened, I began to laugh as I figured out that my uncle was unfortunately forced to turn down a date with a beautiful flight attendant.

CHAPTER FOUR

My uncle and I sat alone in a conference room at CNI headquarters. We had been dumped there immediately after our arrival. The room was lavishly furnished. We looked across a broad rich brown and polished table at each other from within soft leather chairs that rivaled our seats in first class. The hospitality was in stark contrast to the furnishings — a half hour had passed before someone even brought us a tray with some beverages.

I sipped some orange juice. "*Tengo hambre*," I said. "Any idea when we'll be allowed to go?"

"Until they figure out who tried to kill us, they're not going to let us leave."

"It goes without saying that this all has something to do with your NSA affiliation."

"It would seem so," he said.

"What does CNI stand for, anyway?"

"*Centro Nacional de Inteligencia*," he said. "National Center of Intelligence."

"*Nacional*," I repeated. "Are all words that end '*al*' the same in both Spanish and English?"

"Just about," he answered. "Always put the accent on the final syllable. So how would you say 'central' in Spanish?"

"*Central*," I said, accenting the '*al*'.

"Original?"

"*Original*," I said, turning the 'g' into a hard 'h'. "How about that word 'Intelligence'?"

"English words that end in 'nce' have '*ncia*' in Spanish. The accent goes on the syllable before the '*ncia*' ending."

"So we're waiting for a *conferencia* with CNI?"

"Good. The same thing, by the way, applies to words that end 'ncy' in English. Turn those into '-*ncia*' too."

"Dependency is *dependencia*?"

"Yes. How about 'urgency'?"

"*Urgencia*."

"You got it."

We both turned as the main door to the conference room opened. The woman we met at the attack entered first, followed by a white haired heavy-set man in a rumpled gray suit. Both were holding manila folders. The woman was carrying something wrapped in red cloth.

"Sorry to keep you waiting, gentlemen," she said. "First off, we've not been properly introduced. I'm Agent Ana García. This is my boss, Director Jorge Rodríguez."

"*Mucho gusto*," I said, shaking hands with each. "*Me llamo Juan Valquist. El hombre es* Dr. Andrew Valquist."

They may have appreciated my Spanish efforts, but my accent was weak enough for them to thankfully keep the rest of the conversation in English.

"I'm sure you're wondering who attacked you earlier."

"It crossed our minds," my uncle said. "You have an answer for us?"

Agent García nodded. "We don't know who shot at you, but we believe we know why they did it."

"Alright," I said.

She unwrapped the object she had brought. I saw a dark metal plate with raised letters on it. She slid it across the table to my uncle.

"What do you make of this?" she asked.

He leaned over and studied the object closely. I could see him mumbling as he looked at it from different angles. He finally sat back.

"Where did this come from?" he asked.

"A utility company found it while digging near the Roman amphitheater at Merida," Rodríguez said. "Luckily they contacted the government before anyone in the public found out what it was."

"So what is it?" I asked.

My uncle leaned over and studied it again. "It would seem to be a clue in Latin to some sort of hidden treasure. But I'm not aware of any notorious hidden treasures in Spain."

"We're glad to hear that," Agent García said. "It means that our government's greatest secret was never divulged."

"Alright," my uncle said. "Let's pull this all together. What's going on and why were we attacked?"

The man nodded. "This bronze plate is a clue to the location of a massive gold treasure that was hidden back in the 1600's. One of the kings of Spain was concerned that the chaos sweeping across Europe could eventually force him out of power. He arranged for the treasure to be hidden and safeguarded by a series of clues. This was all arranged by a group of Dominican friars who then, unfortunately, were killed by bandits on their way back to the palace."

"Ouch," my uncle said.

"And the fact of this hidden treasure has been kept a secret and passed down to successive governments to the current day," she said. "But without a clue to follow, there has been no way to recover it."

"So that still doesn't explain why someone tried to kill us," my uncle said.

"We've had this thing for two weeks and no one here at CNI has been able to figure out what the clue means," the man said.

I smiled and entered the conversation. "Then the well-known Latin scholar and former intelligence officer Dr. Andrew Valquist shows up in Spain. Someone who wants this treasure for themselves was afraid that you've all brought in a heavy hitter."

My uncle nodded. "I think you've got it, John."

"That's what we're thinking too," the man said.

"But I'm here with my nephew to work on Spanish. Who in your office even knew I was arriving?"

"Well, you won't be surprised to learn that your name triggered an automatic alert in our office as soon as you bought your tickets. I'm sure the same thing happens in the U.S. when a known intelligence officer from another country comes for a visit."

"That I can neither confirm nor deny," my uncle said. "So how did you know that we were in danger?"

"While studying your file, I spotted that someone in our office accessed the information without authorization. This concerned me enough to want to talk to you. As it turns out, these people really aren't fooling around."

"Alright," my uncle. "I can see where we're at and how we got here. What happens now? If we leave Spain immediately, are we going to be safe?"

"We assume so," the man said. "But Agent García is proposing a different approach."

"¿Qué es eso?" I asked.

"The events of today show us that this treasure has become something dangerous," she said.

"That's true enough," my uncle said.

"We're hoping you will help us locate it. Until it is found and safely in government control, we're concerned that what happened today could just be the beginning of violence."

"I'm going to need some time to talk to my nephew alone, if you don't mind."

The two CNI agents got up from the table.

"We'll be waiting down the hall," she said.

They left the room.

I could see a deep concern in my uncle's eyes as he looked across the table at me.

"This isn't exactly how our Spanish trip was supposed to go," he said. "What they're asking me to do is a dangerous matter."

"It's also important," I said. "And I know that if they tried to kill you once, they'll go after you again. But I understand that this is something you need to do. I can be on the next plane home."

He looked at me startled. "I'm not doing this without you. We go home together or we stay together. But you need to know that this is indeed very dangerous stuff."

I smiled. "I was so hoping you would let me stay."

"Then we've decided?"

"*Sí, mi tío.*"

"And it goes without saying that we don't tell your mom and dad about what we're doing," he said, standing from the table.

"They're on their cruise by now," I replied. "What they don't know certainly won't hurt them."

My uncle stepped to the door and opened it. "You can come back in," he called out.

The agents returned and took their seats.

"I will assist the Spanish government in locating this treasure, but I do have a few conditions."

"Alright," the man said. "Such as?"

"For starters, my nephew comes with us. Who else is on the team from your side?"

"Just me," Agent García said. "We want to keep a very small fingerprint on this thing from our office."

"And what about Agent Rodríguez?" I asked. I looked at the man. "No offence."

"None taken," the man said. "I'm the director of CNI. Maybe I didn't make that clear earlier."

"We can trust him," my uncle said. "My other condition is that we bring in a friend of mine who happens to be in Spain, Dr. Alfred Witter."

"We know all about him," Agent García said. "An MI-5 agent whose Latin scholarship rivals yours. Even though it doesn't look like the hostiles know about him, we've got him under surveillance for his own protection."

"This team needs him," my uncle said. "What I don't know he probably will."

She nodded slowly. "That makes sense. I'll send someone to get him. We've got accommodations set up for you here in the building. For your own safety, you will not be leaving here alone."

"But doesn't someone in this building want my uncle dead?" I asked. "Is this place really safe for him?"

"We've used metadata to identify thirteen possible agents who could be involved in the information breach," the director said. "They're all now out of the building on administrative leave and under house arrest until we figure out which one or ones were involved in this. So I assure you, you're all quite safe from here on out."

"In that case, will we be able to get our stuff from the hotel?" I asked. "Tomorrow morning I need something from my uncle's briefcase."

"I would have thought you'd be more concerned with when they're going to feed us!" my uncle said, laughing.

"I'm beyond hungry," I said. "But I do need to keep up on my studies."

"I apologize," Agent García said. "Yes, we will bring all your things here. And a lunch will be catered in to your rooms as soon as you get settled in."

My uncle pushed his chair away from the table. I followed suit and we both stood.

"When you go get Dr. Witter, just tell him that Andy needs him to repay a favor. He'll understand and should come without trouble."

"Yes, Dr. Valquist," she said. "Now, if you'll both follow me, I will show you to your rooms. After Dr. Witter arrives, we'll hold a full briefing and plan our next move."

My uncle and I sat at a table in his suite. My room across the hall was just a little smaller, so we used his for our hang out. In front of us were empty dishes that had recently held various foods.

"I'm stuffed," I said. "I don't know what half of this stuff was, but I loved it."

"Welcome to your first taste, literally, of Intelligence work. The reality is, we live pretty good."

"So tell me more about this Dr. Witter who's arriving," I said. "Where did you meet this guy? What favor does he owe you?"

"The unclassified way to say where I met him would be that it was at 'an overseas facility'. The favor he owes me is that I saved his life. So helping us find a lost treasure is letting him off easy."

"I'm going to admit, *mi tío*, that the only thing I won't like about this is that you and I won't get to share as much time together."

He looked at me seriously. "I understand what you're saying, John. And I'm going to be very sensitive to that. In retrospect, I should not have invited Maria the flight attendant to dinner during our vacation."

"I'm not saying that was wrong," I said. "I enjoy our visits and I just hope we still get time, is all."

"We're still going to be studying a lot of Spanish together every day. And you're not a third wheel on this expedition."

"Thank you."

"How do you say 'expedition' in Spanish?"

"*Expedición.*"

"Good. There's something else I want to talk to you about. No matter what Director Rodríguez says, we've been shot at today and someone out there wants me dead. I can't stress enough that there is danger in this."

"I understand that."

"What kind of training did your dad give you growing up?"

I looked at him in confusion. "Training? What do you mean?"

"Like where'd you learn to pitch so well?"

"He taught me how to throw rocks when I was little. When I started playing Little League, I found out those skills worked just as well with a baseball."

"Didn't you ever wonder why your dad knew how to throw rocks so well?"

I was puzzled by the question. In retrospect, it did suddenly seem strange that my father, an Orthodox priest, had an uncanny talent for throwing rocks at targets. And for some reason he instilled this skill in his son. As a pitcher on a full scholarship, I'm happy he did, but now I wonder why he taught me in the first place.

"So where did my dad learn to throw rocks?"

"Your grandmother taught him."

"Alright," I said, chuckling. "And why did my grandmother know how to hit a tree at thirty feet?"

"Or hit a communist agent," my uncle said.

"Oh boy," I said. "Are you trying to tell me that my grandmother was some kind of freedom fighter back in Romania?"

"She was. And she passed down those skills to us. Look, I'm not going to tell you any more, that's your dad's job. He must have his reasons for not sharing this all with you. But since you and I are now going into an operation together, I wanted you to know that if something happens, you should follow your instincts. Without you even knowing it, you've been trained a considerable amount in the fighting arts."

"That remains to be seen," I said. "Did you ever use these skills?"

"I used them all the time," he said. "Remember, I was a soldier in Afghanistan. After that I was an NSA agent for four years before returning to teaching."

"What about my father?"

"We had an adventure once, he and I," my uncle said. "But that's for another time." He took out a pen, scribbled something on a piece of paper, and slid it across the table. "Put this in your wallet."

"What is it?" I asked, picking it up and looking at a strange series of numbers.

"It's a phone number for you to call if some emergency develops on this expedition."

"This doesn't even have a valid country code," I said.

"The person who answers will know that it is Dr. Andrew Valquist that needs help. Just keep that safe in case you need it."

I took out my wallet and stuffed away the slip of paper. "You're not really a 'former' agent, are you?"

He looked at me and smiled, shaking his head slowly. I realized he was avoiding any more out loud discussion of this.

There was a knock at the door.

"*Adelante*," my uncle said.

"What is this nonsense, Andy?" asked a tall bald man, storming into the room. "This Spanish agent wouldn't tell me anything. I had a very interesting dinner date lined up. So this better be good."

As he walked toward us, Agent García also entered the room, carrying a large laptop case.

My uncle rose and hugged the man. "It's good to see you, Al. For the sake of your plans, I'm sorry it had to be a day early, but I believe you'll be happy I called."

The man turned to me. "You must be John." He shook my hand. "How's the Spanish coming?"

"*Así así*," I said.

"*Bueno.* Alright, tell me why I'm here, Andy."

"I'll take care of that while we start trying to solve the first puzzle," Agent García said, connecting her lap top to a computer projector she took from the case.

She quickly explained to Dr. Witter what had happened and what we already knew. She then projected a large image of the bronze tablet on the wall. "We believe this Latin phrase somehow points to the treasure or more likely, based on the story passed down, to more clues before we can find the treasure."

Dr. Witter read it outloud. "*Tempora fluentes tenentis claves custodiunt viam ad thesaurum. Hic viam assumere potestis.*"

Agent García cleared her throat. "Our translators have rendered it as 'Times flowing are holding the keys which guard the road to the treasure. Here you can take up the road'."

"You should fire your translators," my uncle said.

"How would you interpret it?" she asked.

"That last part was okay. But the first part should be read as 'Flowing times of the one holding the keys guard the road to the treasure'."

"And that's so different?"

"Little differences do matter," Dr. Witter said. "Andy, remember that time someone at CIA translated an Arabic 4th form verb as if it were 6th form?"

"Yeah. We're just lucky no one got hurt," my uncle said.

"Flowing times," I said. "As in the sands of an hourglass?"

Everyone turned to look at me.

"Very well done, John," Dr. Witter said. "I think you've solved that part. But how does an hourglass or sand hold the key to this puzzle?"

"If somebody had paid attention better in catechism class, they wouldn't be asking that question," my uncle said.

"Right," I added. "It's who's holding the keys. St. Peter obviously."

Again they all looked at me.

"Why did you invite me along, Andy?" Dr. Witter asked. "Your nephew's doing great. So what are we saying this means? Hourglass of St. Peter?"

"Of course!" Agent García exclaimed. "Arenas de San Pedro. It's a town about a hundred kilometers west of here. It means, literally, the Sands of St. Peter."

"And that area somehow guards the road to the treasure," my uncle continued. "That must mean the location of next clue."

"How do we find this clue?" I asked. "It's probably buried somewhere just like the first one.

"But it's probably on a similar or identical bronze tablet," Agent García said. "They intended these clues to last."

"Well, we can't exactly go through the whole town with a metal detector," my uncle said.

"We won't need to," Dr. Witter said. He took a PDA from his suit jacket. "Your friends at MI-5 have the niftiest toys of any Intelligence Agency. This thing not only has all my MP3's on it, but it's a metal detector. I can tune it to the shape and consistency of the tablet we have and it'll locate similar objects within ten yards."

"So we needed you after all," my uncle said, smirking.

Agent García projected a map of central Spain on the screen. She began focusing in and soon we were looking at the town of Arenas de San Pedro.

"Any ideas of where to start?" she asked.

"The first clue was found near a Roman ruin, right?" I asked. "So maybe the next one will be near something Roman as well."

"That's a good idea," she said, typing on the computer. She pulled up several screens. "It looks like the closest thing to a Roman ruin in the town is something called the Roman Bridge."

"Notice on the map that the main church in town is *Nuestra Señora de la Asunción*," my uncle said. "I would guess that's where the clue is buried. The verb *assumere*, 'to take up', was a clue to the location, since the word *Asunción* is derived from the same root."

"Honestly, it doesn't matter," Dr. Witter said. The town's small enough that my detector will locate a bronze tablet if we're even close. Let's start at the bridge and then go to the church if necessary."

She turned off the projector. "Then it sounds like we have a plan. I propose we rest up and head out early tomorrow. Let's say eight in the morning?"

"That'll give me time to study Phase Four before we leave," I said.

"I'll have supply requisition us a vehicle," she continued. "Let's hope there aren't too many clues to follow."

We all stood from the table.

"Good evening, then, gentlemen," she said, starting to smile. "I believe an enemy has unwittingly helped us form a winning team here."

CHAPTER FIVE

I awoke the following morning to the surprise that I had slept through the entire night. Pulling my watch toward me, I squinted and saw the time.

"Five-thirty," I whispered to myself. "*Es tiempo para* Phase *Cuatro*."

Agent García had shown me how to phone for any services I needed. I dialed the number and heard an immediate answer.

"*¿Sí? ¿En qué puedo servirle?*" a voice said.

"*Buenos días,*" I said. "*Yo quisiera café, por favor.*"

"*En seguida, señor.*"

I heard a click. For a moment I worried that they didn't know who I was, but then remembered that I was in the headquarters of an intelligence agency and that they at least could see the extension I called from.

Knowing my coffee would arrive soon, I had the energy to start into my studies:

Phrases

It's 1:00.
   Es la una.

It's half past nine.
   Son las nueve y media.

It's a quarter to seven.
Son las siete menos cuarto.

Seeing how time is told in Spanish, I said out loud the time I had woken up. "*Son las cinco y media.*" Fifteen minutes had passed since then and I now knew how to say the current time. "*Son las seis menos cuarto.*"

I continued studying the time:

It's ten to five.
Son las cinco menos diez minutos.

It's 8:24 exactly.
Son las ocho y veinticuatro minutos en punto.

I wrote out and read aloud all these sentences, practicing to myself how to change the numbers and tell different times. I was ready to start in on the nouns when I began to wonder where my coffee had ever gone. A knock at the door relieved my concerns.

"*Sí,*" I said, opening to a man holding a tray laden with cups and condiments and a white plastic coffee decanter.

"*Aquí está su café, señor.*"

"*Gracias,*" I said, pointing at the desk where I was working.

He set the articles down, nodded to me, and quickly left.

I sucked down a quick cup, feeling the infusion of caffeine from the first sip. This sent me back with renewed energy to the nouns:

Nouns

the neighbor
el vecino

the bed
la cama

the room
el cuarto

the book
el libro

the paper
el papel

the pen
el bolígrafo

the car
el coche

the school
la escuela

the job
el trabajo

the building
el edificio

the telephone
el teléfono

the money
el dinero

Food and Drink

the plate
  el plato

the fork
  el tenedor

the glass
  el vaso

the knife
  el cuchillo

the cup
  la taza

the spoon
  la cuchara

the napkin
  la servilleta

I noticed that my new vocabulary was moving beyond very basic words. I was becoming worried that this batch was too much to really learn in one sitting. So I contented myself with just writing them out and reading them aloud, knowing that I didn't have to master all these immediately. I figured I would also learn some of them just in the course of conversations.

I pressed forward into adjectives:

Adjectives

married
  casado

interesting
  interesante

sure	afraid
seguro	*miedo*
fast	busy
rápido	*ocupado*
slow	angry
lento	*enojado*
some	ready
unos	*listo*
excellent	
excelente	

Looking over all the words I had learned so far in Phase Four, I was encouraged by items such as *teléfono* and *rápido*, where adding an '*o*' to what I knew in English would have been close to the right answer. I imagined that in any sentence where I made up a Spanish word and even came close to the real word, a Spanish speaker would still understand me and just think that I mispronounced the Spanish word.

"Bravery and creativity," I whispered, as I continued through the nouns:

I wrote out the words and took a break to have another cup of coffee. It was approaching seven o'clock and I realized I wouldn't be able to finish Phase Four before our planned eight o'clock departure. My memory of the map, however, told me that I would have time in the car to finish up before we arrived at our destination.

Another knock at my door had to be my uncle.

"*Adelante*," I said, remembering my uncle had said that once to invite someone to enter a room.

"*Buenos días*," my uncle said, carrying a cup of coffee. "*¿Cómo estás esta mañana?*"

"*Bien*. I've gotten a lot done already this morning, but I'm going to have to finish up Phase Four in the car."

"*Eso no es un problema*," he said.

"So how late did you and Dr. Witter stay up last night?"

He finished his cup of coffee and refilled off my decanter. "Only until about one. He kind of needed to talk. It turns out that he and his wife are getting a divorce. Don't tell him I shared that with you."

"Understood. In light of his reference to going on a hot date, I'm not surprised. Are we all having breakfast before we head out?"

"Yeah. In fact, Agent García phoned me to say that we would eat back in the conference room. It should be ready by now. After that we'll hit the road."

"What should I bring with me?"

"She'll have a big vehicle, so bring everything. If we do find the next clue, I'm betting it directs us somewhere far enough away that we won't be back in Madrid tonight."

"Damn, this is going to be fun!"

"So let's get some food and then go on an adventure."

We took our bags down the hall and rode an elevator to the conference room. Agent García and Dr. Witter were already there.

"Help yourself to whatever you would like," she said, scooping eggs onto her own plate.

"*Gracias*," I said, sitting down next to her. From that angle, I had my first opportunity to study her closely. She was an attractive woman in her mid-thirties with a small nose and faint freckles. Her curly brown hair was pulled back into a short pony-tail held with a red ribbon. Today she was wearing khaki slacks and a bright white blouse. I noticed that she did not have a ring on her left hand.

Before eating, my uncle crossed himself in our Orthodox style. I followed suit, a bit embarrassed that I had already stuffed a roll in my mouth.

"*¿Y cómo está Usted esta mañana, Agente García?*" my uncle asked.

I saw her face light up at his attention. "*Muy bien. Y, por favor, llámeme Ana.*"

"*Y propongo que todos nosotros usemos las formas familiares*," my uncle said. "*De acuerdo?*"

"*Sí*," Dr. Witter said.

"*Claro*," she said.

"What did we just agree to?" I asked.

"We're going to use the familiar forms together," she said.

"The *tú* form on your verb list," my uncle said.

"And call me, Ana, not Agent García."

"*Yo soy Juan.*"

"*Y soy* Al," Witter said.

"*Yo soy* Andrew. *Solamente* Al *me llama* Andy."

The two men laughed.

After taking our fill of the breakfast foods, Ana stood first.

"I'll be downstairs in front of the building in ten minutes. Just put your things in the minivan and get in. Obviously don't talk about our mission in the halls."

"Gotcha," I said.

"*Hasta pronto*," she said and departed quickly.

My uncle sat back and stretched his hands above his head. "How are you feeling today, Al?"

"I've been better," he said. "I think I didn't need that last glass of wine last night."

"We probably didn't need that whole last bottle."

Al turned around and double-checked the closed door. "Um, if I'm not mistaken, a certain attractive Spanish spy has a little case of the Andy's."

"What are you talking about?" he asked.

"I saw it too," I added. "When you asked her how she was doing, the air rose ten degrees on this side of the table."

"You guys are crazy," my uncle said. He looked up slowly. "Are you serious?"

"Just don't blow this like you did with that Russian consular official," Al said.

"You know as an NSA agent I couldn't pursue that. I would have had to report her as a 'close and enduring relationship'."

"But you're not NSA anymore, are you?" Al said.

We stood and grabbed our bags to head out.

"Let's just concentrate on the mission," my uncle said. "We don't need complications."

"This is the spice of life," Al said. "Just see how things evolve."

A short elevator ride brought us to the main lobby. We exited the building and saw a white minivan parked alone in front. Al opened the trunk and we loaded our things in. I slung my carry-on over my shoulder, which contained my notebook and Phase Four.

Al and I purposely jumped quickly into the back seat, forcing my uncle to sit up front. He shot us a quirky look when he realized our motive.

"Just ignore me for a while," I said to all. "I've got about an hour of study left for today."

"I think it's terrific that you're working so hard," Ana said. "And with a teacher as wonderful as your uncle, I know you'll do great."

I could see in my peripheral vision that Al was suppressing a chuckle. As the rest chatted about Madrid landmarks along the way, I returned to Phase Four:

Time

Sunday
domingo

Monday
lunes

Tuesday
martes

Wednesday
miércoles

Thursday
jueves

Friday
viernes

Saturday
sábado

the season
la temporada

the spring
la primavera

the summer
el verano

the autumn
el otoño

the winter
el invierno

Prepositions

under
debajo de

on
sobre

over
por encima de

next to
junto a

into	inside
en	*dentro de*

than	outside
que	*afuera de*

I decided to both practice my Spanish and stoke the fires a bit.

"*Perdóneme, mis amigos,*" I said," *Pero quiero preguntar algo.*"

"*Sí?*" Ana answered. "*¿Cómo podemos ayudarte?*"

"I'm confused by something. The adjectives for tired and married are so similar. I mean, *cansado* and *casado*. That's crazy. Is there a good way for me to remember the difference?"

"Just remember that the one with only the 's' means married," Al said.

"And what does the 's' stand for?" I asked.

"Sick of being married," he said with a laugh.

"I wouldn't know about that," Ana said.

My uncle scoffed. "I was going to suggest that the one with an 'n' can remind you of 'night' and that's when you're usually tired."

Al and I smiled at each other in the mutual recognition that Ana had managed to clarify her single status in the conversation.

"That helps," I said. "Alright, I'm going back to work."

I studied the expected section of miscellaneous words:

Miscellaneous

yet/still	far
todavía	*lejos de*
each/every	during
cada	*durante*
before	in order to
antes de	*para*
after	probably
después de	*probablemente*
near	
cerca de	

More numbers followed:

Numbers

thirty	fifty
treinta	*cincuenta*
forty	sixty
cuarenta	*sesenta*

seventy	thousand
setenta	*mil*
eighty	first
ochenta	*primero*
ninety	second
noventa	*segundo*
hundred	third
ciento	*tercero*

I headed into my verbs. I had the full forms of more important items:

Basic Verbs

ir, to go

I go	we go
yo voy	*nosotros vamos*
you (sing. informal) go	you (pl. formal) go
tú vas	*Ustedes van*
you (sing. formal) go	they go
Usted va	*ellos van*
he/she goes	
él/ella va	

hacer, to do/make

I do/make
   yo hago

we do/make
   nosotros hacemos

you (sing. informal)
do/make
   tú haces

you (pl. formal)
do/make
   Ustedes hacen

you (sing. formal)
do/make
   Usted hace

they do/make
   ellos hacen

he/she does/makes
   él/ella hace

hablar, to speak

I speak
   yo hablo

we speak
   nosotros hablamos

you (sing. informal)
speak
   tú hablas

you (pl. formal) speak
   Ustedes hablan

you (sing. formal)
speak
   Usted habla

they speak
   ellos hablan

he/she speaks
   él/ella habla

decir, to say

I say
  yo digo

we say
  nosotros decimos

you (sing. informal) say
  tú dices

you (pl. formal) say
  Ustedes dicen

you (sing. formal) say
  Usted dice

they say
  ellos dicen

he/she says
  él/ella dice

Even though this looked like a lot, I was becoming more comfortable with the verb endings, so it wasn't really new material. Finally, I had a few more infinitives of valuable verbs:

Verb Infinitives

to enter
  entrar

to write
  escribir

to exit
  salir

to look
  mirar

to read
  leer

to sit
  sentarse

to stand	to find
estar de pie	*encontrar*
to forget	to lose
olvidar	*perder*
to remember	to bring
recordar	*traer*

The car was big and solid enough that I was able to legibly write out all the materials even though we were now racing on open highway. As I finished my work, I looked out the window and saw rising mountains in the distance.

"*¿Dónde estamos?*" I asked.

"We've got about another fifty kilometers to Arenas de San Pedro," Ana said.

"How's the Spanish coming?" my uncle asked.

I chuckled. "Sometimes I'm thrilled to realize I can say an entire sentence in Spanish when I need it. Other times I feel like an idiot when I go to say something and don't know half of what I need."

"That's how it is," Al said. "The first time I visited Romania with your uncle I worked hard to learn a little of that crazy language. At a restaurant I went to order potatoes and instead of asking for *cartofi* I asked for *pantofi*. Awfully similar words."

"What do they mean?" Ana asked.

"My friend asked for an order of fried shoes," my uncle answered.

"Which is what I think the steak at that place really was," Al quipped. "Just keep doing exactly what you're doing, John. You'll have breakthroughs and setbacks, but as long as you keep regularly studying, you'll keep making progress."

The horizon slowly evolved into brown and gray mountainous ridges, with green brush glaring against the arid landscape along the road.

"This is the area I saw from the plane," I noted.

"So we came out here after all," my uncle replied. "With any luck you'll still get the chance to relax on the beach before the trip is done."

We began to see signs counting down the distance to our destination. After a half an hour, we saw a large blue overhead sign announcing the upcoming exit for Arenas de San Pedro.

"I'm going to just head straight for the Roman Bridge," Ana said.

"Sounds good," Al said. He took out his PDA and started pressing buttons on the display.

"So what else does that gadget do?" I asked. "Or would you have to kill me if you told me?"

"Nah. It's a phone, quite encrypted at that. It's a metal detector, which you know. It's basically a powerful computer with everything you need, including the internet."

"And being a British device," my uncle started. "It also gives terrible haircuts and makes unpalatable food."

"Wow," I said. "You're just going to let that go?"

"I made fun of a Romanian steak, so I think we're even." He continued pressing buttons. "I've got the bridge mapped out. It's clear on the opposite side of town as we'll enter it."

"*Gracias*," Ana said.

We pulled into Arenas de San Pedro and immediately were creeping through two lane residential roads lined with tan stone buildings. We finally made our way to the western outskirts of the town. The so-called Roman Bridge crossed a river off the road. Ana parked our vehicle and we all headed toward the site.

"I feel lucky," Al said, holding his PDA and leading the group. "Like I said, I should be able to locate a bronze table like the other one very easily." He walked slowly to the entrance of the bridge and turned periodically to each side. Reaching the opposite end of the stone structure, he continued several yards down the path. He finally turned to face the group.

"I want to widen the search a bit, but this really may not be the place."

My uncle sighed. "I was hoping we would find it quickly. Especially since I'm starving."

Al took his device and began exploring a wide perimeter around the area of the bridge. The rest of us leaned against the stone wall in the middle of the bridge.

"It's a beautiful area," Ana said, running a hand through her hair in the gleaming sun.

I walked off the bridge, thinking my uncle might be nervous talking to her directly in front of me. Towards the east, I could see a castle of tan stone overlooking the city from a central hill. Looking quickly over my shoulder, I could see my uncle seeming to make nervous small talk with Ana.

Al finally returned from his efforts after twenty minutes.

"I'm afraid we'll have to go search elsewhere. I'm just not picking anything up."

Andrew nodded. "We should try the church area next. I did think that was the place. But we also can't dismiss the possibility that the clue is here and the metal detector just isn't working."

Al held out his hand and showed several coins. "It found all of these. I think this is enough to buy lunch for the team."

"That's encouraging," Andrew said. "I'm hungry, but I propose we keep going."

"Agreed," Ana said, heading for our vehicle. "To the church!"

Al gave directions and within just a few minutes we were standing in front of *Nuestra Señora de la Asunción*. Crowds of tourists were coming in and out of the church.

"Digging up something discretely may be difficult here," Andrew said.

"All I have to do is flash my badge and we can do whatever we want," Ana said, smiling at him.

We walked as a group, pretending to look at the building while Al scanned the area with this PDA. When we reached the back of the building, we saw a group of fairly young trees.

"I hope the clue wasn't dug up by landscapers at some point and thrown away," I said.

"It wasn't," Al said.

"How can you be so sure?" Ana asked.

"Because I'm standing directly above it."

"Really?" Andrew said excitedly.

He turned the display on the device toward us. We could see an image in the same shape as the original clue.

"My device says that whatever this is, it's made of bronze and is two feet down."

"I've got a shovel in the back of the van," Ana said. "One of you go get it while I explain to the priest that we're conducting government business out here."

I ran and got the shovel. As I was returning to the spot, Ana was returning, followed by a bald man dressed in the same long black cassock my dad wears.

"*Aquí tenemos que excavar, Padre*," she said.

"*No comprendo*," the priest said. "*Qué creéis que encontraréis allá?*"

"*No puedo decirle, Padre,*" she returned. "*Es un secreto de estado.*"

She gave me a nod and I started to dig. Al monitored the depth and soon advised me to start digging by hand. As my fingers pressed downward, I felt the sudden coldness of metal. I squeezed my fingertips around one side and pulled the object loose. Sitting back, I pulled out a dirt covered metal plate.

"*Tengo que pedirle que salga, Padre,*" Ana said. "*Hemos encontrado lo que buscábamos.*"

"*Sólo limpiad este lugar un poco,*" the annoyed priest said, waving his hands at the hole. Even I understand that he wanted me to at least put the dirt back where it was.

I refilled the hole and patted the dirt down while Andrew and Al gently wiped the dirt off the plaque and took the first look at the artifact.

"It's definitely another clue," Al said. "It's corroded enough that we will have to very delicately clean it up before we can get a text off it."

"Listen," Ana said. "We're all very hungry and most likely the clue is going to be leading us to another location. Even if we solve it quickly, we'll have to put off our forward travel until tomorrow."

"That makes sense," I said.

"My government will pay for hotel rooms here. Let's get dinner and then get settled."

"*Buena idea,*" I said.

We sat in Ana's hotel room after a relaxing dinner. Al and Andrew had cleaned up the plaque and arrived at full consensus on the Latin inscription. Ana's computer was projecting the text onto one of the walls.

My uncle read the text outloud, "*Locus de unde aquae veniunt ductae vobis monstrabit viam.*"

Al translated for us. "The place from which the waters, having been led, come will show you the path."

"I'll give you an A+ for that," Andrew said.

"*Gratias ago tibi,*" Al answered in Latin.

"Sounds kind of vague," I said. "The place the waters come from?"

"This is easy," Al said. "You need to move *ductae* back next to *aquae*, which it is modifying. *Aquae ductae*. I'm betting this is a reference to the rather famous Roman aqueduct at the city of Segovia."

"Nicely done," Andrew said. "And can we find out where those waters originate?"

"I'm on it," Ana said, typing on her computer. A minute later she posted an internet page on the wall. "The source of the waters for the Segovia Aqueduct is a site twelve kilometers south of the city."

"And where is Segovia?" I asked.

"It's about a hundred and twenty kilometers northwest from here," Ana said. "It's north of Madrid, but we'd go through Avila from where we are now."

"A very doable trip tomorrow morning," Andrew said.

Al stood up and started toward the door. "I'm really starting to feel the lateness of last evening. So I'm going to turn in early, people."

"Shall we say eight o'clock again?" I asked.

"It's a good plan," Ana said.

After Al left the room, I realized I was now the only thing preventing my uncle and Ana from being alone.

"I want to read through all the phases I've done so far, *mi tío*," I said. "So I'm going to my room. See you all in the morning."

"*Buenas noches*," he said.

"*Hasta mañana, Juan*," Ana said with smile, looking not at me but my uncle.

Chapter Six

I again woke up before the sun. Even though I was still quite tired, I knew I wasn't going to successfully fall back asleep. I looked at the clock on the night stand.

"*Son las cuatro y cuarto,*" I whispered.

My uncle had warned me that one could experience disrupted sleep even four days into a major time change, so I decided to not fight it and just get started studying for the day. Unfortunately I also knew that I would not have access to coffee until six when the hotel restaurant opened for our free continental breakfast.

Phase Five phrases came first:

Phrases

I want to speak with you for a moment.
   Yo quiero hablar contigo por un momento.

I will try to answer that question for you.
   Yo voy a tratar de contestar esa pregunta por ti.

He went to Spain in order to study Spanish.
   El fue a España para estudiar español.

The second phrase reminded me that I can use the verb 'to go' to form the future tense. I continued into the phrases:

115

He went to Spain in order to study Spanish.
She left early because she was tired.
   Ella salió temprano porque estaba cansada.

If you want, you can come with me.
   Si quieres, puedes venir conmigo.

Let's go to the museum now.
   Vamos al museo ahora.

My eyes were getting bleary from both fatigue and lack of coffee as I continued into the nouns:

Nouns

the problem
   el problema

the city
   la ciudad

the question
   la pregunta

the street
   la calle

the answer
   la respuesta

the light
   la luz

the language
   el idioma

the mail
   el correo

the difference
   la diferencia

the letter
   la carta

the address
  la dirección

the airplane
  el avión

the opportunity
  la oportunidad

The volume of new words was way more than I could learn without coffee, but I at least wrote them out.

Phase Five words just kept coming and made me hungry for a breakfast that was still a half an hour away:

Food and Drink

the pepper
  la pimienta

the fruit
  la fruta

the salt
  la sal

the beef
  la carne de res

the meat
  la carne

the chicken
  el pollo

the potato
  la papa

the fish
  el pescado

the vegetable
  la verdura

I took all my materials with me and went downstairs to the restaurant. My uncle was already waiting at the door for the place to open.

"*Buenos días, mi tío,*" I said.

"*Buenos días. ¿Cómo dormiste?*"

I did not know the verb ending he used, but the verb itself meant to sleep. I guessed at his question. "*Bien. ¿Y tú?*" I decided to imitate his question with a different twist. "*¿Cuándo dormiste?*"

"We stayed up a while and talked." He looked at me and sighed. "I admit that I'm becoming conflicted about Ana. She's a beautiful and intelligent woman who is obviously signaling an interest in me."

"What's wrong with that?" I asked.

"I just don't know that I need this type of complication in my life right now. Not to mention that we're in the middle of a strange little historical pursuit that requires all my concentration."

I hugged my uncle. "Do whatever seems right to you, no matter what that is. I just want you to be happy."

"*Gracias.*"

Through the glass doors, we saw a worker inside the restaurant begin setting up carafes of coffee and trays of pastries. He finally came and unlocked the front door.

"*Después de tú,*" I said.

"*Gracias.* But it's *después de ti.*"

"Okay, so the correct form for 'after me' would be *después de mí?*"

"*Sí.*"

"I rule."

We got inside and poured cups of coffee. While my uncle read a newspaper, I continued studying:

Adjectives

important	different
importante	*diferente*

"How many English words that end with 'nt' have '*nte*' in Spanish?" I asked, looking up from these words.

"Enough that you can add it to your creative creations list. How do you say 'instant'?"

"*Instante.*"

"Fluent?"

"*Fluente.*"

"How about 'excellent'?"

"*Excelente.*"

"*Bueno.*"

I continued into the adjectives:

hot	necessary
caliente	*necesario*
cold	difficult
frío	*difícil*
interested	easy
interesado	*fácil*

same	smart
mismo	*inteligente*
possible	stupid
posible	*estúpido*
impossible	other
imposible	*otro*
early	next
temprano	*próximo*
late	last
tarde	*último*
clean	right
limpio	*cierto*
dirty	wrong
sucio	*falso*

We drank several cups of coffee and ate a few rolls as I studied and my uncle read the newspaper. Phase Five gave me more prepositions:

Prepositions

between	about
entre	*sobre*

until	in front of
hasta	*enfrente de*
around	against
alrededor de	*contra*
without	instead of
sin	*en lugar de*
behind	
detrás de	

The Miscellaneous section was mercifully short:

Miscellaneous

both	like
ambos	*como*
finally	suddenly
finalmente	*de repente*
almost	too (much)
casi	*demasiado*
if	so
si	*tan*

The end of Phase Five presented more verbs and infinitives:

Basic Verbs

dar, to give

I give
yo doy

you (sing. informal)
give
tú das

you (sing. formal) give
Usted da

he/she gives
él/ella da

we give
nosotros damos

you (pl. formal) give
Ustedes dan

they give
ellos dan

pensar, to think

I think
yo pienso

you (sing. informal)
think
tú piensas

you (sing. formal) think
Usted piensa

he/she thinks
él/ella piensa

we think
nosotros pensamos

you (pl. formal) think
Ustedes piensan

they think
ellos piensan

vivir, to live

I live
   yo vivo

we live
   nosotros vivimos

you (sing. informal) live
   tú vives

you (pl. formal) live
   Ustedes viven

you (sing. formal) live
   Usted vive

they live
   ellos viven

he/she lives
   él/ella vive

Verb Infinitives

to love
   amar/querer

to help
   ayudar

to send
   enviar

to look for
   buscar

to teach
   enseñar

to work
   trabajar

to learn
   aprender

to call
   llamar

to study	to try
estudiar	*tratar de*

to hope	to sleep
esperar	*dormir*

After writing everything out and reading it over one last time, I set my pen down and rubbed my eyes. "My brain is getting full. I have to make sure I have coffee before I start Phase Six tomorrow."

"There is no Phase Six," he said.

"What? How do I keep learning?"

"From here, you just practice what you've learned and keep learning new words you need in real life. That and do your homework."

I saw Ana coming through the door of the restaurant. She was wearing a long blue skirt and a striped red and blue blouse. Her hair cascaded in luxuriant brown curls past her shoulders. From her appearance, you might have guessed she was going on a date rather than overseeing a dig in Segovia.

"*Buenos días, hombres*," she said, sliding into the booth beside Andrew.

The delicate fragrance she was wearing swirled around us. I knew that my uncle did not stand a chance of avoiding this complication.

"*¿Cómo están Ustedes?*"

"*Estoy muy bien*," I answered. "*Y tú?*"

"*Muy bien*." She accented the *muy* as if to signal some particular happiness in her life.

Al emerged through the door of the restaurant. "*Buenos días a todos*."

"*Buenos días*, Al," Andrew said. "*Dormiste bien anoche*?"

"*Sí*. I'm feeling much better today."

We ate breakfast, checked out, and continued our trip. The city of Segovia was about a hundred and twenty kilometers away, but the highway to get there was smaller than the road that took us from Madrid to Arenas. As a result, we were pressing into the afternoon before we finally arrived at our destination.

"I've got the specific place mapped out for us," Al said. "After we enter Segovia, you'll be heading out of town on the south side and from there we've got just twelve kilometers."

"And this time it doesn't seem there's any argument about where to look, right?" I asked.

"From what I can see on the internet, the source of the aqueduct is a known spot. It has a structure made in Roman times to pull water off this mountain stream and start it into the aqueduct system."

Andrew turned around from his now accustomed seat in the front with Ana. "*¿Cómo se llama el lugar?*"

"It's the Río Acebeda," he replied. "We can also expect it to be a little touristy."

We arrived in Segovia. As we made our way into the center of the city, we saw the massive aqueduct itself, towering proudly over the modern buildings around it.

"I can't believe the Romans made something that big," I said.

"You need to see the Coliseum in Rome," my uncle said.

We left the city and continued down a small road toward the source. We pulled through the small village of Revenga and after several more kilometers, the road turned into a narrow lane and finally stopped altogether.

"We'll have a little less than a kilometer on foot to get the place," Al said.

I got out and grabbed the shovel from the back. "With any luck we'll be getting lunch back in that little town in no time."

We continued on a foot path marked by crude signs pointing the way. Al informed us that, in addition to Segovia having one of the best preserved ancient aqueducts, the structures at the source were reportedly impressive. We walked quickly, from a combination of both excitement and hunger. We saw other hikers both ahead of us and behind.

As we approached the actual site, we saw large blocks of stone, obviously carved in ancient times. Al took out his PDA and began walking around the area. Within one minute he stopped and turned to us.

He was smiling broadly. "Bingo!"

As I came over and started digging in the spot where he pointed, I noticed that other tourists were looking at us curiously. Rather than show credentials, Ana seemed to be relying on the small number of people just assuming that our little group was on official business.

"You're getting close," Al said. "Do the rest by hand."

Just as at Arenas de San Pedro, I dug a few more inches through soil and felt the plate. I pulled it out and handed it to Ana.

"We know it's what we came for," she said. "Let's just head out and process it later."

In what was almost becoming a routine, we were relaxing in Ana's hotel room in Segovia after dinner. Al and Andrew looked at an enlarged image of the artifact which Ana projected on the wall.

"*Prope aquam sex augustae ordines stant et spectant viam*," Al read outloud.

"Near water, six august orders stand and watch the road," Andrew translated.

"I concur on the translation," Al said. "But I don't know what this one means."

Ana brought up an internet window. "Any ideas on what to search for?"

"Is it possible *orders* here is a reference to religious orders?" I asked. "I mean, the guys who hid these clues were monks."

"*Ordines* is the word used in Latin to describe such orders," Al said.

"As well as every other use of the word 'order' you can imagine," Andrew added. "But it's certainly worth exploring."

Ana typed on her computer. "I'm looking for a place near water which might have six monasteries?"

"Water could be a reference to the Mediterranean," Al said.

"Or the Atlantic," Ana said. "Or a little stream for that matter. And probably every village in Spain has at least one monastery in it."

"But the number six is the real clue," Andrew said. "Surely there has to be a town with exactly six of them."

"We're on the wrong track here," Al said. "Even if we locate a town that had six different religious orders at the time these clues were buried, there's still the matter of finding a buried plaque. Remember that the monks didn't envision a British agent with a metal detector. They intended people to be able to follow these clues and have at least a rough idea of where to dig in the ground."

"He's right, John," my uncle said

"My idea's not panning out," I said. "So what else comes in orders?"

Ana typed something into her search. "I'm just entering *Roman* and *orders*." She hit return and we all saw the results.

"Of course," Al said. "The number two result is about Roman Catholic religious orders. But the first return is about the different orders of Roman columns."

"So orders here could mean a collection of columns that sits somehow notably by a body of water," Ana said. "But that still leaves much of the Mediterranean coast."

"These monks didn't go that far," Andrew said. "Look at what we have so far. The clue starts in Mérida, took us to Arenas de San Pedro, and then on to Segovia. They haven't left central Spain yet. Let's look for a collection of columns somewhere near a lake or a river."

Ana continued entering various words into searches. Nothing seemed to bring satisfactory results.

"Maybe we need to step back here a bit," my uncle said. "If we know that the next clue is somehow near a Roman ruin in central Spain, let's look at a map of Roman settlements to see if something pops out at us."

"Good," Ana said, changing the search. She located a map and projected it for us to study.

"Hey," Al said, standing and pointing to a spot on the wall. "There's a settlement named Augustobriga. That would make sense of the reference to "august orders." Let's run a search on place."

Ana entered the word and hit return.

"Go to images," I said.

We cheered as we saw multiple photos of a Roman ruin with exactly six columns beside a river.

"Alright," my uncle started. "It looks like we've solved this one. How far a trip is that from here?"

Al played with his PDA for a moment. "That's going to be a four hour drive."

"I'm tired of taking a day off every time we manage to solve these things," Ana said. "How about we bail on this hotel right now, drive down there, and get in a hotel somewhere closer?"

"I like it," my uncle said. "We know exactly where we're going, so we could even look for the clue yet tonight."

"Pack up, people," she said. "Let's move."

CHAPTER SEVEN

The sun was getting lower in the sky and blinding us on our westward journey. While our team was certainly excited to be going to the location of another clue, it had been a long day already. Al fell asleep shortly after we passed by Madrid. I sat studying Phases One through Five quietly but could not help listening in on my uncle and Ana as they talked. I did not understand all of it, but the overall tone of the conversation told me that my uncle was losing the grip on his heart.

"*Es interesante*," he said. "*Te he conocido sólo por unos días, pero parece más tiempo.*"

"*Comprendo*," she said, looking at him and smiling sweetly. "*Y voy a admitir que ya no quiero que nuestro tiempo juntos vaya a acabarse.*"

"*¿Qué hacemos después de encontrar el tesoro?*"

"*Nosotros? Quieres decir — tú y yo?*"

He was quiet and took a breath as if building his courage before jumping off a cliff. "*Sí.*"

She nodded. "*Una parte de mí sabe que en una experiencia como ésta el estrés hace que nos sintamos más cerca uno del otro. La verdad es que quiero abrazarte y besarte.*"

Al stirred and began to stretch, which ended their conversation. I was even a bit relieved that I could ask about a word I saw in my list.

"*Mi tío, dígame algo*," I said.

"*Sí?*"

"I noticed that the word *oportunidad* is so close to the English word opportunity. Can I assume that all words in Spanish that end with *–dad* are the same as English words with *–ty?*"

"*Absolutamente,*" Al said. "Would you like me to give you a language drill?"

"If you don't I know my uncle's going to."

"How do you say capacity in Spanish?"

I converted the word. "*Capacidad.*"

"Infinity."

"*Infinidad.*"

"Electricity?"

"*Electricidad.*"

"And they're all feminine in gender."

The sun had now fully set. We continued on for three more hours, the lights of oncoming cars become more and more scarce. Before we left, Al had entered our route on his PDA. We would head south when we saw an exit for a town called Peraleda de la Mata. From there it would be just ten kilometers until we reached the ruins we believed guarded the next clue. As we continued driving, Al read us more background information on the site. We learned that the six pillars were on the south bank of the Río Tojo. They were called *Los Mármoles*, or "the Marbles." This was due to the misconception that they were made from marble, when in fact they were granite. To our horror, however, he informed us that the large body of water to the northeast of Los Marmoles had been produced by the construction of a dam only in 1963, which created a reservoir of water which buried the ruins of a sizable Roman city there. We were hoping against hope that the treasure was not hidden in that city.

It was nearly ten o'clock at night when we arrived at Los Mármoles after crossing a bridge over the Rio Tojo. In silence we got out of the vehicle. I grabbed the shovel and followed the group. Al was already waving around his PDA by the time we stood before the lumbering pillars of the ruins. They were glowing in the light of the moon and threw intersecting shadows on the ground below us.

"Got it," Al said quietly.

I began to dig.

"We're lucky none of these clues were ever accidentally found by the various archaeological teams that have explored around these ruins," Andrew said.

"They've tended to be deep enough that they wouldn't be found by ordinary landscaping," Al said. "But you're right, any one of them could have been found. It's our fortune that they weren't. That's good. Dig by hand from here."

I got on my knees and suddenly wondered how and when I had inherited the job of being the chief excavator. I suppose being the youngest one of the team made me the obvious choice. I wasn't complaining. The metal plate came out easily. I handed it to my uncle.

He wiped away the dirt. "Since there's no one around, let's try to read it here."

"Yes," Al said, shouldering up to him and studying the thing.

Ana and I watched as the two Latin scholars examined the clue. I could see in each of their faces that there was something very different about this plaque. They spoke in low tones to each other and nodded, pointing at different words. Finally they lowered the artifact. Both were smiling brighter than the moon.

"This doesn't seem to be a riddle," Andrew said. "It's describing the location of the treasure."

"And it's not that far from here," Al added.

"What does it say?" Ana asked excitedly.

My uncle looked at the plaque and translated. "What you seek is five miles to the north. It is under the ancient bridge."

"But it doesn't actually say the treasure is there," I noted. "It could be that this is just a really transparent message for how to find the next clue."

"That's possible," Al said. "But this is so different from all the rest of the clues we've seen that I think this is the end of the journey."

Ana stepped backward a few feet from the group. "Do you think you can locate the bridge using your PDA?" she asked.

"Checking that now," Al said. A second later he nodded. "Here it is. There's a Roman bridge just five hundred meters south from the main highway we just came off. The distance seems right."

"So where does that leave things?" she asked.

I noticed that Ana took another step backward.

Al put his PDA in his coat pocket and walked toward her. He turned suddenly, with a pistol drawn and pointed at me and Andrew.

Ana reached into her shoulder harness and took our her pistol and also aimed it in our direction.

"What is this, Al?" my uncle said in confusion.

"You and John just stay over there and don't try anything stupid." He turned to Ana. "It was murder watching you flirt with him."

"I know," she said, leaning over and kissing him quickly. "But it had to be done."

My brain raced, trying to figure out what was taking place.

"Throw me your phone, Andy," Al said, menacing him with the gun.

My uncle complied and tossed the device over to him.

"Wouldn't want you somehow contacting any former friends for help." He pocketed my uncle's phone and then looked up at us seriously. "Now get moving down the road," he said, pointing with his gun.

As my uncle started walking, I caught up with him.

"What's happening here?" I asked.

"It seems these two are together on a plan to take all this gold."

"What do we do?"

"For now, we have to do everything they say. They've got two guns and we have none. But you need to get a stone."

"What?"

"Alright, no talking," Ana said.

I caught up to his thinking. "Yes, I understand." Even as I said the words, my stomach turned at the thought that I might have to hurt someone. My next spasm of worry came from the concern that getting a rock without being seen would be difficult and potentially dangerous. I decided to do nothing rash and wait for a clear moment.

"Get in that barn over there," Al said, pointing past us with his gun.

We turned toward a wooden building I hadn't even noticed when we arrived. It was sun baked and only flecks of an original coat of red paint still clung here and there. Andrew opened the wide front door and let me step in first.

"Now why don't you tell me what you're doing?" my uncle asked, blocking the door.

I immediately knew that he was giving me a moment to find a stone. I dropped to one knee and ran my hand along the ground, feeling the shape and consistency of several candidates. I finally grabbed two nearly spherical stones and quickly pocketed them.

"Get in there," Al bellowed.

My uncle walked backward and joined me on the other side of the barn. Rude wooden rafters crossed far above us. Scattered along the walls were broken glass windows at eye level. The faint odor of cow manure and hay clung to the space all around us. Ana and Al stood at the door, the moonlight managing to illuminate the inside of the structure well enough to see even their faces.

"You do at least deserve an explanation," she said. "Al and I met at an intelligence briefing about a year ago and fell in love. When I learned that the first clue had been found, I knew our future together depended on us getting that treasure. So we needed to find a way for me to get assigned to that case."

"That's when you gave us the perfect way in, Andy," he said. "When I found out that you were coming to Spain, I created this plan for the staged attack."

"That was you in the car?" I asked.

"*Sí*," he said. "And it gave Ana a reason to bring you in and propose her plan to the director."

"But how did you know I would want you involved in this project?" Andrew asked.

"A hidden treasure? Latin clues to decipher? You wouldn't have wanted to do it without me, right?"

"And indeed I didn't," he said. "In other words, you counted on my loyalty and high esteem for you in a plan to stab me in the back."

"Your bad," Al said.

"Alright, so what happens now?"

"I'm going to guard you two here," Ana said. "Al's going to go confirm with his PDA that it's a ton of gold under that bridge and not yet another clue that we may need your expertise to interpret."

"And why should my uncle help you now?" I asked.

"To keep from watching a bullet go between your eyes," Al said. "So shut up."

"Al," my uncle said. "Is our friendship worth nothing to you?"

"Not as much as a couple hundred million dollars," he said. "Alright, I'm leaving. Ana."

"Hurry, my love," she said. The two locked in a deep kiss.

"Awkward," I said.

"I'll be right back," he said, going out the door.

Ana closed the doors to the barn behind him and leaned against them, her gun pointed at us.

"Ana, when you and Al have the gold, you can let us go," my uncle said. "There's no reason to kill us."

"You and I both know that's not how these things turn out."

The sounds of the van kicking up gravel slowly moved away. My memory told me that we had driven for only fifteen minutes after leaving the main highway. That meant that Al could potentially check out the spot and be back here in a half an hour.

My heart pounded so hard that I was sure my uncle and Ana could hear it. And my mind focused on the round rock in my pocket. I estimated Ana's distance from me to be about half that of the mound to home plate. It would have been better if she were a little farther away.

"We need to face the fact that we are in trouble," my uncle said. "Do you get the *pitcher*?"

He had distinctly pronounced his words, though I suspected that Ana didn't catch the difference. My uncle was signaling that it was time to act. He started to walk slowly toward Ana, drawing her attention to himself.

"Ana, my heart is broken by what you've told me. My feelings are real."

My hand found the rock and I gently pulled it from my pocket.

"Andrew, let it go," she said. "You know that the old 'pretending to have feelings to distract a target' routine is the oldest trick in the spy manual. I just can't believe you fell for it."

"Fell for it? I fell in love with you."

She rolled her eyes in disgust. I would never have a better shot.

I pulled my arm back quickly. As I threw the rock forward, I saw her eyes dart from my uncle toward me. All the way to my fingertips, I was controlling the speed and direction of the stone. It entered the air between us and I was pulled off my own feet by the momentum.

The stone painted a streak through the air and struck Ana directly on the forehead. The barn echoed with the sound of a sickening crack, followed by the blaring of a gunshot.

As I landed on my hands and knees, I saw both Ana and my uncle collapse to the ground.

"Damn it!" I screamed, getting to my feet and running toward my uncle. As I moved, I glanced over and saw that Ana was completely unconscious on her back. I crouched beside my uncle.

"I'm fine," he said. "She got me in the leg, is all." He quickly took off his shirt and tied it directly over a wound pouring blood from his thigh.

"What should I do?" I asked.

"You have to go get help," he said. "I saw on the map that there's a town to the south of us down this main road. Between here and there you might even find a farm house. You still have that number I gave you?"

"Yes, but can't we defend ourselves with Ana's gun?"

"I'm in no condition to fire a gun well enough to face him," he said. "And I know you can't beat Al in a gun battle. You have to do this, John. Get going."

"I can use Ana's phone!" I said frantically.

"No," my uncle said, shaking his head. "They didn't mention calling each other. I worked with Al and know how he operates. Any call from her phone will alert him that something's wrong."

"Alright," I said, getting up from the ground.

"Give me Ana's gun," he said. "I'll need it in case she wakes up. But you need to get assistance before Al returns."

I picked up her gun and handed it to my uncle.

"*Vaya con Dios*," he said, his eyes welling with tears.

I knew this phrase from somewhere. "Go with God." It was a way to say goodbye, but my uncle meant it literally.

I raced out the door and started running down the road. The moon had risen in the sky and now lit up the night. Only then did I feel the bracing chill as my face, drenched in sweat from the ordeal, was drying in the air as I moved. I had run about five minutes when I suddenly felt the panic that Al could be returning in just another fifteen and I still had not located help. As I rounded a turn, I saw the lights of a farmhouse just off the road. I ran to the front door of the house and knocked hard several times.

"*¿Sí?*" I heard from inside. "*¿Quién es?*"

In the panic of the moment, I almost automatically returned a sentence in English. I took a deep breath and tried to pull together everything I had learned in the previous several days.

"*Perdóneme, señor. Yo necesito ayuda. Tengo una* … (how do you say emergency in Spanish? Oh, right, just convert '-ncy' to *ncia*) *emergencia. Necesito usar su teléfono.*"

The door opened. A grizzled man wearing dirt soaked overalls stood in front of me. "*¿Cuál es el problema?*" he asked.

"*Mi tío es* (how do you say hurt? How do you say injured? I'll just say sick) *enfermo. Muy enfermo.*"

"*Voy a llamar una ambulancia,*" he said, taking out a cell phone.

(Ambulance. No, I need to use that phone.)

"*Lo siento, señor, pero necesito usar su teléfono. Es* … (It's an absolute necessity). *Es … una necesidad absoluto.* (Darn, I should have used a feminine adjective.)

He looked in my eyes carefully and I would like to think that despite my disastrous attempts at Spanish what he ultimately understood was my sincerity. (Which would be *sinceridad* in Spanish, in case you ever need it.)

"*Está bien,*" he said, handing me the phone.

"*Muchísimas gracias,*" I said, quickly entering the number my uncle gave me.

On the other end was the strangest ring tone I have ever heard. Then came a click.

"Dr. Valquist?" a voice said with concern. "What's wrong?"

"This is Dr. Valquist's nephew," I replied. "He's hurt and we need help immediately."

I heard some frantic typing. "What kind of help do you need?"

"Medical and ... well, military. In ten minutes a man is returning who intends to kill us."

"Where are you relative to Dr. Valquist?" the voice asked.

"A few kilometers down the road," I said.

"You need to get this phone back to him."

"Why?"

"Because I'm going to use it as a beacon to locate you."

"You can do that?"

"Even the police can do that," the voice said. "But you are talking to the NSA, you know."

"Okay, but this isn't my phone. I borrowed it from a farmer."

"Put him on the line," the voice said.

I handed the phone to the man. *El quiere hablar con Usted.*

The man put the receiver to his ear and started to nod. "*Sí,*" he said. "*Sí. Sí, comprendo. Está bien, le paso el teléfono al joven.*"

He handed me back the phone.

"What did you tell him?" I asked, putting the phone back to my ear.

"I told him that the United States government will be giving him one million dollars if he lets you take that phone right now."

"You're really going to do that?"

"For Dr. Valquist, yes." the voice said.

"So I guess you speak Spanish, huh?"

"This is the NSA, kid. Now go, you need to get that phone back to the place you left him. I'm getting CNI on the line to send help."

I looked up at the farmer. "*Gracias, señor,*" I said, the words almost catching in my throat.

He nodded. "*Vaya con Dios.*"

I looked in his eyes. As I smiled, tears ran down my cheeks. I turned and started to sprint back up the road.

By that moment I had lost all concept of time. Had I been at the farmer's house for one minute or five? Did I attack Ana one minute after Al left or was it five? All of this together meant that I didn't know if Al could be back already or if I still had time to make it there.

None of it mattered, though. I just kept running with all the strength I had. The road I had travelled just a few minutes before did not seem familiar to me. But I pressed forward, starting to feel waves of nausea as I exceeded my body's ability to oxygenate fully. And it didn't help that we were in an altitude significantly higher than Cleveland. At one point, I went into a full gag, still managing to throw one leg in front of the other as I doubled over with waves of pain and spasmed muscles in my midsection.

A sense of euphoria exploded within me as I suddenly saw the barn in the distance and no sign yet of the minivan. Spots were forming before my eyes as I reached the door. I staggered inside and saw my uncle sitting on the ground, his injured leg stretched out in front of him. He was holding the gun on his lap and pointing it at the corner of the barn. I turned and saw Ana sitting upright, conscious.

"Did you do it?" he asked.

I nodded, still catching my breath.

"You bastard," Ana said. "When Al gets back here, I'm going to personally kill both of you."

I continued pulling deep breaths into my lungs and sat down on the barn floor next to my uncle.

"Where did you find a phone?" he asked.

"Way down the road," I said, still gulping air. "A farmer."

"Farmers in central Spain don't tend to speak English."

"So I found out," I said, still catching my breath.

"But you spoke to him in Spanish and managed to call my emergency number."

I chuckled and looked at him. "*Sí, mi tío. Hablo con él en español y llamo tu número de emergencia.*"

"This idiot nephew of yours doesn't even know the past tense," Ana said.

"He'll have time to learn it while you're spending the rest of your life in prison," he said.

Just then we all heard the sound of tires crunching gravel in the distance. It grew louder and then ground to a halt.

"Or maybe he won't live to learn the past tense," she said, picking herself up from the barn floor.

"Can't you just shoot him as he comes through the door?" I asked, not even believing that such words could be coming out of my mouth.

"We had an agreement," she said. "If I don't come outside when he returns, he knows that you somehow have a weapon."

"Give me my orders, uncle," I said. "I'm ready to die, but not without a fight."

My uncle shook his head. "This is not a fight you and I can win, John. All we can do is hope and pray."

"What's going on, Ana?" Al called loudly from outside the barn. "He's got a weapon?"

"They've got my gun," she shouted. "Take them!" She looked at Andrew. "Say your goodbyes to your nephew."

"This is your final warning, Andy," Al shouted. "Let Ana come out."

Just then, the sound of helicopter rotors pierced the distance. At first it was hard to make out the direction they were coming from. Then I realized there were many and they were coming from everywhere.

"You're surrounded, Al," he shouted. "You better drop your weapon and have your hands up when those snipers see you. You've got only a second to do that!"

"Damn you!" Al screamed.

The barn door burst open. We saw the shadowy silhouette of Al raising his pistol toward us.

I winced, expecting shots from his gun. In the next split second, several high pitched noises shrieked from every direction. A red vapor exploded from Al's body as he fell backward, landing on the gravel covered ground at the entrance of the barn.

Ana ran toward him.

"Don't!" my uncle shouted.

She knelt beside Al and grabbed his gun. Ana turned and lifted it toward us. Bullets again screamed through the air. As she stared at us, her hand slowly dropped. A look of deep sadness came upon her as she slowly slumped onto the ground.

CHAPTER EIGHT

I stretched out on my lounge chair. My legs were still sore from the sprint for my life I had made just two days earlier. Forty feet forward I saw the gentle bluish-green waves of the Mediterranean lap against a shore of smooth golden sand. People filed by in the strong sun of the late morning. In European manner, some of them were taking up the clothing optional style.

"*Tengo hambre, mi tío,*" I said. "*¿Cuándo quieres comer?*"

My uncle put down some local tabloid he had picked up at our hotel. "*Ahora,*" he said.

I saw him shift his weight on his chair, favoring the right leg that carried a cast. The bullet had managed to nick his femur, prompting such measures. He raised his hand and snapped his fingers.

"*Sí, señor,*" a hotel attendant said, instantaneously appearing.

I rolled my eyes, still uncomfortable with the level of service at a five star hotel.

"*Estamos listos para el almuerzo,*" he said.

The young man took out a notepad and looked at us eagerly.

"*Para mí,*" I started. "*Yo quisiera una hamburguesa y papas fritas.*"

"*Y para beber?*"

"*Una limonada,*" I replied. "*Con mucho hielo.*"

"*Y para el señor?*" the man asked.

He chuckled. "*La misma cosa.*"

"*En seguida, señores,*" the man said, making a quick retreat toward the hotel.

"*Dígame algo, Juan,*" my uncle said.

"*Sí?*"

"Do you realize that entire conversation was in Spanish?"

I nodded slowly. "*Sí,*" I said. I searched my brain for things I was able to say in order to construct another sentence. "*Ahora yo puedo decir muchas cosas.*"

"*Y dígame algo,*" he continued. "*Puedes hablar español?*"

I thought about his question a moment. The answer had to be no. I was still surrounded every instant by proofs that I did not know Spanish perfectly.

"*No, mi tío. Ahora todavía no puedo hablar español.*"

"*¿Qué dices?!*" said a female voice on the other side of my uncle.

I turned toward her and found my eyes immediately in a flutter at the sight of a beautiful young woman in a purple bikini.

"*Obviamente hablas español,*" she said.

"*Gracias,*" I returned. "*Pero* ... (I thought through what I knew) *ahora solamente yo sé palabras* ... (how to say basic? Just put a Spanish ending on the English word) *básicas.*"

She laughed. "*Hablas español. ¿Cómo te llamas?*"

"*Me llamo Juan,*" I said.

My uncle struggled forward and stepped up from his lounge chair. "I'll be back in a few minutes," he said.

"*¿A dónde vas?*" I asked him in a whisper.

"Out of the way," he said.

Our eyes locked in a recognition of all we had been through in the last week.

"*Mi tío ...* " I started, then didn't know what more to add.

"*Yo sé*," he said, smiling.

PHASE ONE: SPANISH

Greetings and Phrases

Hello
  Hola

Goodbye
  Adiós

See you later
  Hasta luego

Good morning
  Buenos días

Good afternoon
  Buenas tardes

Good night
  Buenas noches

Please
  Por favor

Thank you
  Gracias

You're welcome
  De nada

Excuse me
  Perdóneme

yes
  sí

no / not
  no

maybe
  quizás

and
  y

or
  o

Do you speak English?
  ¿Habla inglés?

I don't speak Spanish very well.
  Yo no hablo español muy bien.

Please speak more slowly.
  Por favor, hable más despacio.

Please repeat that.
   Por favor, repita eso.

I'm sorry, but I don't understand.
   Lo siento, pero yo no lo entiendo.

How do you say that in Spanish?
   ¿Cómo se dice eso en español?

What does that word mean?
   ¿ Qué quiere decir esa palabra?

Basic Verbs

I am
   Yo soy / Yo estoy

I have
   Yo tengo

I like
   Me gusta / Me gustan

I need
   Yo necesito

I want
   Yo quiero

I can
  Yo puedo

I go / I will
  Yo voy

I know
  Yo sé

I think that
  Yo creo que

Could you ... ?
  ¿Podría Usted ... ?

I'd like...
  Me gustaría...

Pronouns

I
  Yo

you (sing. informal)
  tú

you (sing. formal)
  Usted

he
  él

she
  ella

we
  nosotros

you (pl. informal)
  vosotros

you (pl. formal)
  Ustedes

they
  ellos

Numbers

number
  número

zero
  cero

one
  uno

two
  dos

three
  tres

four
  cuatro

five
  cinco

six
  seis

seven
  siete

eight
  ocho

nine
  nueve

ten
  diez

PHASE TWO: SPANISH

Phrases

What is your name?
  ¿Cómo se llama Usted?

My name is ...
  Me llamo ...

Nice to meet you.
  Mucho gusto.

How are you?
  ¿Cómo está Usted?

I'm fine
  Estoy bien

So-so
  así-así

Where are you from?
  ¿De dónde es Usted?

I'm from ...
  Yo soy de ...

Where is the ...
  ¿Dónde está ... ?

What time is it?
  ¿Qué hora es?

How much does that cost?
  ¿Cuánto cuesta eso?

Where do you live?
  ¿Dónde vive Usted?

I live in the United States.
  Yo vivo en los Estados Unidos.

I'm an American.
  Yo soy americano.

Nouns

the man
  el hombre

the woman
  la mujer

the person
  la persona

the thing
  la cosa

the place
  el lugar

the chair
  la silla

the table
  la mesa

the house
  la casa

the bathroom
  el cuarto de baño

the name
  el nombre

Food and Drink

the food
  la comida

the drink
  la bebida

the water
el agua

the bread
el pan

Adjectives

good
bueno

bad
malo

nice
simpático

pretty
bonita

handsome
guapo

sick
enfermo

tired
cansado

happy
  contento

sad
  triste

right
  derecha

left
  izquierda

this
  esto

that
  eso

big
  grande

small
  pequeño

Time

the time
  el tiempo

the hour
  la hora

the day
  el día

the night
  la noche

the morning
  la mañana

the afternoon
  la tarde

the evening
  la tarde

yesterday
  ayer

today
  hoy

tomorrow
  mañana

now
  ahora

then
  entonces

Interrogatives

who
  quién

what
  qué

where
  dónde

when
  cuándo

why
  por qué

how
  cómo

how much
  cuánto

how many
  cuántos

Prepositions

in
en

with
con

to
a

of
de

from
desde

for
para / por

Miscellaneous

here
aquí

there
allí

really
  de veras

very
  muy

also
  también

but
  pero

together
  juntos

well
  bien

again
  otra vez

of course
  por supuesto

Numbers

eleven
once

twelve
doce

thirteen
trece

fourteen
catorce

fifteen
quince

sixteen
dieciséis

seventeen
diecisiete

eighteen
dieciocho

nineteen
diecinueve

twenty
veinte

twenty-one
veintiuno

Basic Verbs

ser, to be

I am
  yo soy

you (sing. informal) are
  tú eres

you (sing. formal) are
  Usted es

he/she is
  él/ella es

we are
  nosotros somos

you (pl. formal) are
  Ustedes son

they are
  ellos son

estar, to be

I am
  yo estoy

you (sing. informal) are
  tú estás

you (sing. formal) are
  Usted está

he/she is
  él/ella está

we are
  nosotros estamos

you (pl. formal) are
  Ustedes están

they are
  ellos están

querer, to want

I want
  yo quiero

you (sing. informal) want
  tú quieres

you (sing. formal) want
  Usted quiere

he/she wants
  él/ella quiere

we want
  nosotros queremos

you (pl. formal) want
  Ustedes quieren

they want
  ellos quieren

tener, to have

I have
  yo tengo

you (sing. informal) have
  tú tienes

you (sing. formal) have
  Usted tiene

he/she has
  él/ella tiene

we have
  nosotros tenemos

you (pl. formal) have
  Ustedes tienen

they have
  ellos tienen

Verb Infinitives

to be
  ser, estar

to do/make
  hacer

to go
  ir

to be able
  poder

to eat
  comer

to drink
  beber, tomar

to speak
  hablar

to say
  decir

to think
  pensar

to know
  saber, conocer

to want
  querer

to need
  necesitar

to have
  tener

to like
  gustar

PHASE THREE: SPANISH

Phrases

My father is a nice man.
  Mi padre es un hombre simpático.

This man is tall.
  Este hombre es alto.

My car is bigger than yours.
  Mi auto es más grande que el tuyo.

I have no idea.
  No tengo ninguna idea.

Are all your friends here?
  ¿Están todos sus amigos aquí?

I learned many things from him.
  Yo aprendí muchas cosas de él.

That woman is beautiful.
  Esa mujer es bonita.

I saw my friend's new house yesterday.
  Yo vi la casa nueva de mi amigo ayer.

Tell me something new.
   Dígame algo nuevo.

I think that this shirt is better than that one.
   Pienso que esta camisa es mejor que ésa.

I'm hungry.
   Tengo hambre.

I'm thirsty.
   Tengo sed.

Nouns

the people
   la gente

the boy
   el niño

the girl
   la niña

the husband
   el marido

the wife
   la esposa

the father
  el padre

the mother
  la madre

the son
  el hijo

the daughter
  la hija

the brother
  el hermano

the sister
  la hermana

the friend
  el amigo

the family
  la familia

Food and Drink

the coffee
  el café

the tea
  el té

the milk
  la leche

the beer
  la cerveza

the wine
  el vino

Adjectives

my
  mi

our
  nuestro

your
  tu

their
su

his
su

her
su

much/many
mucho/muchos

few
pocos

all
todo

none
ninguno

new
nuevo

young
joven

old (people and things)
viejo

more
  más

less
  menos

better
  mejor

worse
  peor

Time

the second
  el segundo

the minute
  el minuto

the week
  la semana

the month
  el mes

the year
  el año

always
  siempre

never
  nunca

sometimes
  a veces

often
  a menudo

once
  una vez

twice
  dos veces

soon
  pronto

Miscellaneous

because
  porque

much
  mucho

a little
  un poco

enough
  bastante

only
  solamente

already
  ya

nothing
  nada

something
  algo

Basic Verbs

saber, to know

I know
yo sé

you (sing. informal) know
tú sabes

you (sing. formal) know
Usted sabe

he/she knows
él/ella sabe

we know
nosotros sabemos

you (pl. formal) know
Ustedes saben

they know
ellos saben

poder, can, to be able

I can
  yo puedo

you (sing. informal) can
  tú puedes

you (sing. formal) can
  Usted puede

he/she can
  él/ella puede

we can
  nosotros podemos

you (pl. formal) can
  Ustedes pueden

they can
  ellos pueden

necesitar, to need

I need
yo necesito

you (sing. informal) need
tú necesitas

you (sing. formal) need
Usted necesita

he/she needs
él/ella necesita

we need
nosotros necesitamos

you (pl. formal) need
Ustedes necesitan

they need
ellos necesitan

gustar, to like

I like
  me gusta/gustan

you (sing. informal) like
  te gusta/gustan

you (sing. formal) like
  le gusta/gustan

he/she likes
  le gusta/gustan

we like
  nos gusta/gustan

you (pl. formal) like
  les gusta/gustan

they like
  les gusta/gustan

Verb Infinitives

to ask
  preguntar

to answer
  responder, contestar

to tell
  decir

to give
  dar

to come
  venir

to see
  ver

to hear
  escuchar

to understand
  entender

to take
  tomar

to use
  usar

to leave
  salir

PHASE FOUR: SPANISH

Phrases

It's 1:00.
  Es la una.

It's half past nine.
  Son las nueve y media.

It's a quarter to seven.
  Son las siete menos cuarto.

It's ten to five.
  Son las cinco menos diez minutos.

It's 8:24 exactly.
  Son las ocho y veinticuatro minutos en punto.

Nouns

the neighbor
  el vecino

the bed
  la cama

the room
  el cuarto

the book
  el libro

the paper
  el papel

the pen
  el bolígrafo

the car
  el coche

the school
  la escuela

the job
  el trabajo

the building
  el edificio

the telephone
  el teléfono

the money
  el dinero

Food and Drink

the plate
  el plato

the glass
  el vaso

the cup
  la taza

the napkin
  la servilleta

the fork
  el tenedor

the knife
  el cuchillo

the spoon
  la cuchara

Adjectives

married
casado

interesting
interesante

sure
seguro

fast
rápido

slow
lento

some
unos

excellent
excelente

afraid
miedo

busy
ocupado

angry
  enojado

ready
  listo

Time

Sunday
  domingo

Monday
  lunes

Tuesday
  martes

Wednesday
  miércoles

Thursday
  jueves

Friday
  viernes

Saturday
  sábado

the season
  la temporada

the spring
  la primavera

the summer
  el verano

the autumn
  el otoño

the winter
  el invierno

Prepositions

under
  debajo de

on
  sobre

over
  por encima de

next to
  junto a

into
  en

than
  que

inside
  dentro de

outside
  afuera de

Miscellaneous

yet/still
  todavía

each/every
  cada

before
  antes de

after
  después de

near
  cerca de

far
  lejos de

during
  durante

in order to
  para

probably
  probablemente

Numbers

thirty
  treinta

forty
  cuarenta

fifty
  cincuenta

sixty
  sesenta

seventy
  setenta

eighty
  ochenta

ninety
  noventa

hundred
  ciento

thousand
  mil

first
  primero

second
  segundo

third
  tercero

Basic Verbs

ir, to go

I go
  yo voy

you (sing. informal) go
  tú vas

you (sing. formal) go
  Usted va

he/she goes
  él/ella va

we go
  nosotros vamos

you (pl. formal) go
  Ustedes van

they go
  ellos van

hacer, to do/make

I do/make
yo hago

you (sing. informal) do/make
tú haces

you (sing. formal) do/make
Usted hace

he/she does/makes
él/ella hace

we do/make
nosotros hacemos

you (pl. formal) do/make
Ustedes hacen

they do/make
ellos hacen

hablar, to speak

I speak
  yo hablo

you (sing. informal) speak
  tú hablas

you (sing. formal) speak
  Usted habla

he/she speaks
  él/ella habla

we speak
  nosotros hablamos

you (pl. formal) speak
  Ustedes hablan

they speak
  ellos hablan

decir, to say

I say
   yo digo

you (sing. informal) say
   tú dices

you (sing. formal) say
   Usted dice

he/she says
   él/ella dice

we say
   nosotros decimos

you (pl. formal) say
   Ustedes dicen

they say
   ellos dicen

Verb Infinitives

to enter
  entrar

to exit
  salir

to read
  leer

to write
  escribir

to look
  mirar

to sit
  sentarse

to stand
  estar de pie

to forget
  olvidar

to remember
  recordar

to find
  encontrar

to lose
  perder

to bring
  traer

PHASE FIVE: SPANISH

Phrases

I want to speak with you for a moment.
   Yo quiero hablar contigo por un momento.

I will try to answer that question for you.
   Yo voy a tratar de contestar esa pregunta por ti.

He went to Spain in order to study Spanish.
   El fue a España para estudiar español.

She left early because she was tired.
   Ella salió temprano porque estaba cansada.

If you want, you can come with me.
   Si quieres, puedes venir conmigo.

Let's go to the museum now.
   Vamos al museo ahora.

Nouns

the problem
  el problema

the question
  la pregunta

the answer
  la respuesta

the language
  el idioma

the difference
  la diferencia

the city
  la ciudad

the street
  la calle

the light
  la luz

the mail
  el correo

the letter
  la carta

the address
  la dirección

the opportunity
  la oportunidad

the airplane
  el avión

Food and Drink

the pepper
  la pimienta

the salt
  la sal

the meat
  la carne

the potato
  la papa

the vegetable
  la verdura

the fruit
  la fruta

the beef
  la carne de res

the chicken
  el pollo

the fish
  el pescado

Adjectives

important
  importante

different
  diferente

hot
  caliente

cold
  frío

interested
  interesado

necessary
  necesario

difficult
  difícil

easy
  fácil

same
  mismo

possible
  posible

impossible
  imposible

early
  temprano

late
  tarde

clean
  limpio

dirty
  sucio

smart
  inteligente

stupid
  estúpido

other
  otro

next
  próximo

last
  último

right
  cierto

wrong
  falso

Prepositions

between
  entre

about
  sobre

until
  hasta

around
  alrededor de

without
  sin

behind
  detrás de

in front of
  enfrente de

against
  contra

instead of
  en lugar de

Miscellaneous

both
  ambos

finally
  finalmente

almost
  casi

if
  si

like
  como

suddenly
  de repente

too (much)
  demasiado

so
  tan

Basic Verbs

dar, to give

I give
  yo doy

you (sing. informal) give
  tú das

you (sing. formal) give
  Usted da

he/she gives
  él/ella da

we give
  nosotros damos

you (pl. formal) give
  Ustedes dan

they give
  ellos dan

pensar, to think

I think
  yo pienso

you (sing. informal) think
  tú piensas

you (sing. formal) think
  Usted piensa

he/she thinks
  él/ella piensa

we think
  nosotros pensamos

you (pl. formal) think
  Ustedes piensan

they think
  ellos piensan

vivir, to live

I live
  yo vivo

you (sing. informal) live
  tú vives

you (sing. formal) live
  Usted vive

he/she lives
  él/ella vive

we live
  nosotros vivimos

you (pl. formal) live
  Ustedes viven

they live
  ellos viven

Verb Infinitives

to love
  amar/querer

to send
  enviar

to teach
  enseñar

to learn
  aprender

to help
  ayudar

to look for
  buscar

to work
  trabajar

to call
  llamar

to study
  estudiar

to hope
  esperar

to try
  tratar de

to sleep
  dormir